Fairy Wars.

A Prequel

by

L. L. Bower, PhD

© 2019 Dr. L. L. Bower

All rights reserved. No part of this publication may be reproduced, stored in a retrieval system, or transmitted in any way by any means, electronic, mechanical, photocopy, recording, or otherwise without the express permission of the author, except as provided by U.S. copyright law.

This novel is a work of fiction. Every name, place, event and description stems from the author's imagination. Any resemblance to real persons, situations, or entities is purely coincidental.

Published in the United States of America

Dedication

To Miss Laub, my high school English teacher, who encouraged me to write and who was the first to get my work published, even if it was only in the school newspaper.

Prologue

Present Day: After I step on the royal fairy and Fairyland and all its creatures are revealed to me, I return to my cabin from a camping trip in the Mansentia forest. I lean my fishing pole against a wall and drop my tackle box on the kitchen table next to a spiral-bound notebook I don't recognize. It's titled *Magic is all around Us* by Calen Bartholomew Ambrose in my handwriting. As I flip through it, some parts are labeled "My Private Notes," and other parts are headed "Chapman's Journal." When did I write all this?

To say I'm shocked at its contents is an understatement. I don't recall some of what it says took place, and I'm hazy as to where the journal went after I finished it. I *do* remember having therapy sessions with Dr. Chapman, and I *do* remember doing some writing for her, but much of the rest is fuzzy. I think the doctor returned my journal when I finished therapy, but where it went after that, I don't know.

Knowing what I do now, however, I believe its contents are all true. I hope whoever reads what follows will better understand my childhood and my destiny, a destiny I never asked for, but one which has changed my life forever.

Chapter 1

My Private Notes. After Session Two with Dr. Chapman.

If anyone would've told me that, at nearly sixteen years old, I'd be seeing a shrink, I'd have called them crazy.

My shrink's name is Dr. Jane Chapman, and she thinks I've blurred fantasy and reality for a long time. The doc thinks I invented Mom's notes about the strange things she witnessed. My sister Cassie, who's three years older, agrees. "I think you made up those notes, to get attention."

But I can still feel the rough papers in my hands and the indent of her neatly written words as clearly as the pen I'm holding.

Problem is, I'm the only one who actually saw those notes. And Mom can't back me up.

Cassie was in the basement with me when the weirdness started, so I asked her to tell the doctor what she saw.

"Calen, I can't help you." She shook her head. "I told her you exaggerated the whole thing. It was a freaky accident, but certainly not supernatural."

"What?! Why are you lying?" I balled up my fists.

"Listen. You're never going to convince that woman of what you saw and –."

"But … but you were at the hospital with me. That part was real."

"I don't think your life was in any real danger." She jutted out her chin.

"I was attacked in my bed! Don't you remember?"

"No." She shrugged. "I don't remember an attack, and that's the truth."

"Great! And the shrink doesn't believe I was even in the hospital.

They have no record of my being there or of a Dr. Gray. My nurse has disappeared and the rest of the employees don't remember me. You're the only one who knows I was there."

"Look. I never wanted to go to therapy to start with. If we tell the shrink what she wants to hear, we can fulfill the state's requirement to get treatment, even though it seems a waste of time."

"So you won't back me up?"

"Nope."

"That's just great!" I groaned. "She's going to think I'm crazy. Won't she put me in a home for whackos or something?"

"Not if you admit you have an overactive imagination. She'll just say you've been through a major trauma, and your mind has altered your memories to help you cope."

I chewed on this for a while and decided she was right.

The doctor has asked me to write down everything I remember because people with PTSD, post-traumatic stress disorder, tend to "repress disturbing events." Having a written record is supposed to help me recognize what's real life and what's fantasy.

To quote her, "Recalling what really happened is the only way to stop your nightmares and panic attacks. Disturbing experiences are like festering wounds. They won't heal until they're opened and dealt with."

When the doc is done reading my journal, I think I'll tell her I invented the whole thing, even though Mom and Dad taught us never to lie. Hopefully she'll believe I'm well, and I won't have to go anymore. And the state will let Cassie and me alone to live out our lives.

I try to ignore the voice in my head. *"But that's still a lie, Calen."*

The doctor said the internal voice I hear from time to time isn't real either. When I looked up "hearing voices," I learned it's a sign of schizophrenia. The voices a schizophrenic hears, however, are loud and commanding. The voice I hear is soft and suggestive.

Here you go, Dr. Chapman:

Dr. Chapman's Journal. June 6, 1991. (My 13th year)

The craziness all started in our dingy, cold basement. Even with the lights on, it was a creepy place. But at the time, I was glad to escape the summer heat, even if the downstairs storage room smelled musty, like old books.

I remember how, in spite of Mom's offer to pay us, I wanted to read, work on the radio I was building or climb a tree, anything but clean out our basement.

But we were moving soon. Dad had just gotten a job teaching at a college in Harrisburg. And Mom said we needed to get rid of the stuff we didn't use.

I should have been excited, right? A new school, a new city, a new house. But I didn't want to move and got a sick stomach every time I thought about it.

That old house was where I lived my whole life, where my sister and I played hide and seek, where we had all our parties, where my best friend lived down the block. It was fearsome to think I'd have to make new friends, leave old friends behind and lose everything familiar.

"Calen." My skinny sister points to a big cardboard box. "You take that one. I'll take this one." She opens another box, one marked in red with "CJA" (for Cassie Joyce Ambrose) "School Stuff." She digs into the box.

"Why are you so bossy?" I make a face at her.

"'Cuz I'm older and wiser." She sticks out her tongue.

"Well, you got the older part right."

Not wanting to be bossed around, I stomp over to the stack of boxes Mom said she wanted to sort through. I grab one labeled "CBA—Baby Stuff." That's me, Calen (with a long A) Bartholomew Ambrose. I set it on the ratty old couch that's pushed up against the concrete wall.

One side of the box has caved in and the top is bowed, like something heavy was piled on it. It's sealed with slightly yellowed tape that's curling at the edges. I pull on the tape and cry, "Yow!"

"You okay?" Cassie doesn't look up from the box she's rifling through.

"Yeah, paper cut." The wound bleeds, and I suck on my finger. The taste of iron fills my mouth. Yuk.

I rip off the tape with my other hand and flip open the top. Stale air hits my nose.

The first thing inside the box is a book with a puffy cover. *Baby's First Book.* A faded-blue baby shoe and Winnie the Pooh decorate the front. Beneath the book are tiny clothes, stuffed animals and baby toys.

Wonder why she kept all this stuff. I'm not a baby anymore.

I hold up the book, smearing it with my blood. "Did you see this?" I ask Cassie.

She smirks. "I've got one too. I think it's so she can embarrass us when we have kids."

"Really? Gross." I'm about to toss the old thing into the "discard" pile, which is much bigger than the "keep" and "donate" piles, when my small internal voice says, *"Look again."*

Sheets of paper in my mom's handwriting hang from the book's middle. I pull them out.

Tossing the baby book back into the box, I plop on the couch to check out the loose pages, which since then, I've studied so much I've memorized them. The first one is dated when I was eleven.

April, 1989.

"I think something weird is going on,"

my mom's notes read. *"Calen has gotten into tight*

situations before, but I thought he was just the kind of boy whose guardian angel works overtime. But today was different. Today he very nearly died."

Huh? I ask myself. *When was that?*

I take deep breaths, feeling like my heart is too big for my chest. I glance at Cassie. She's studying a piece of paper in her hands.

I steady the pages and read on.

"I can't believe what I saw and still wonder if I hallucinated. Perhaps by recording all the strange things that have happened to him in his short life, I'll make some sense of it."

Another date follows.

"Find something interesting to read?" Cassie asks.

"Just some old notes."

"Let me see." Cassie reaches for the pages.

No way is she going to find out that Mom thinks I'm weird. I'd never hear the end of it.

"No!' I yell and hide the pages behind my back.

Cassie jumps. "Okay, okay, chill out."

My heart thumps, and my palms sweat. But I can't let her see how freaked out I am. "It's just baby stuff." I try to sound calm.

"Then get busy! Remember, we don't get paid 'til we finish the job." She throws a stick-figured drawing from her box on top of our ever-growing discard pile. I want to make fun of her silly art, but I'm too upset.

"Yeah, yeah." Folding the notes, I cram them into the back pocket of my jeans. Even though I really want to learn more about my weird life, I need to think about what I've just read and study the rest by myself.

I've always believed I was different. But what does it mean when even my mom thinks so?

After tossing the baby book on the discard pile, I scrounge through the rest of the box. But my heart still pounds. I can't stop thinking about being a strange kid.

For sure I've always been nerdy. I enjoy reading the dictionary and disassembling things to see how they work. When I was younger, I sometimes couldn't put stuff back together, like my remote-controlled car or my "Rock 'em, Sock 'em Robots."

But I got better at the re-assembling part. I took apart Dad's old watch, cleaned its tiny pieces and fit them back together. When the repaired watch actually ran, I don't know who was more surprised, my parents or me.

I hurl the stuffed animals, toys and baby clothes from the CBA box on top of the donate pile. Smashing the box with my foot, I add it to the stack of twenty or so flattened boxes we've already gone through.

The good boxes, the undamaged ones, go in another stack Mom said she'll refill with the "keep" pile.

Together, my sister and I tackle a gazillion more boxes, none as interesting as my baby box. We sort through old toys, faded grade school art, essays on "How I Spent My Summer Vacation" and crinkled *Highlights* magazines. *Does my mom ever throw anything away?*

We also discover boxes of really old college textbooks, my dad's, their covers sun-faded and inscribed with "Mort Ambrose."

In one box, I find Halloween costumes my mom made, some of which I sort of remember wearing, like the red Superman cape. In another box are yellowing newspaper articles Mom wrote when she worked as an editor for a newspaper.

I skim one report called "No Bullies Allowed" by Eloise Cramden (her maiden name) 'til Cassie interrupts my concentration. "Calen, quit slacking off." She tosses her long dark hair over one shoulder to emphasize her point.

With a growl, I leave the box of Mom's articles for her to sort.

The costumes and books are tossed into the donate pile, and the toys, essays and art get thrown on the discard stack, which is almost as tall as I am.

By the end of the morning, we've emptied about two-thirds of the boxes. I'm relieved we'll be done sometime in the afternoon. Tomorrow, I have baseball practice.

After all, doesn't Mom realize this is my summer break? Emphasis on break.

From upstairs, Mom calls, "Lunch!" I empty the box I've started, an undamaged one and put it near the keep pile with the other good boxes.

Mom told us she'll sort through the discard and donate stacks, before anything gets tossed or given away. I'm guessing she has different ideas about what *real* junk is.

I hope she doesn't keep the baby book.

€ € €

We eat lunch on our shaded patio. I dig in with enthusiasm, surprised at how hungry I am and that tuna sandwiches could taste so good.

Mom starts pouring lemonade into each of our glasses. "How's the basement coming?" The ice makes popping sounds when the liquid hits it.

"Great," Cassie answers. "We've cleaned out about thirty boxes. We'd be further along if Calen didn't stop to read everything."

"Really?" Mom gives me a puzzled look. "Like what?"

My throat tightens, and I jump in before Cassie has a chance to respond. "I found some old article you wrote about bullying in schools. It was good." Which isn't a lie, but it isn't the whole truth.

I'm not ready to reveal that I found her notes. After all, they were in a box *she* wanted to sort through, maybe because she doesn't want me to read them.

"I'll probably throw those old articles away." Mom takes a bite of her sandwich.

Before taking another bite, I say, "I thought maybe you'd want to keep some of it."

She peers at the ceiling. "I have all that stuff backed up on floppy disks. Besides, that was my other life. I don't miss the late nights, the deadlines."

"But you still love to write, right?" I emphasize the last two words and laugh, pleased with my rhyme.

My mom, who actually gets my sense of humor, grins. "Yeah, and I still submit freelance stories. But I'm no longer on deadline."

€ € €

After lunch, Cassie and I race to the bathroom. She gets there first and I'm forced to wait outside.

According to Dad's old watch, which I now wear, a minute has passed so I knock on the door. "Hurry up."

Mom's notes feel like they're literally burning a hole in my pocket.

Finally, after what seems like forever, Cassie throws open the door. "Your turn."

"You took long enough."

She flips back her hair and makes a face. I slip in through the open door, close it and turn the lock.

Alone at last, I pull the handwritten pages from my back pocket and sit on the toilet, lid down. Picking up where I left off:

December 22, 1978. (I was a few months old.)

> "I went to check on Calen because he was late waking from his nap. Ever since he was born, I've been afraid something bad might happen to him because I almost lost him twice during my pregnancy. Once I fell, but my doctor said the fetus seemed unhurt. I also went into labor much too early, and no one knew why. The doctor was able to stop the birth pains, but I had to go to bed until Calen was full-term.
>
> "Anyway, when I walked into his darkened nursery with its Winnie the Pooh nightlight, I saw something strange. A shadow, darker than the unlit room, hung

over the end of his crib. Fear filled my mouth. I swallowed hard and ran to him.

"When I reached the crib rail, I looked over it. Calen was gasping for air like a fish out of water. 'Oh my God!' I yelled.

"I switched on the light by his bed. His face was blue. I screamed again and tried to pick him up, but was forced back against the dresser. At first, I thought I'd lost my balance and reached for him again. This time, I was shoved hard to the floor. As scared and shaky as I was, nothing was going to stop me from reaching my child. I tried to rise, but strong, invisible hands pinned me to the floor.

" 'My baby!' I screamed. If I could get to him, I could give him mouth-to-mouth. I flung a prayer heavenward. 'Please help my little boy.' Immediately, a blinding flash of light split the darkness, and Calen began to wail. At the same moment, the pressure on my shoulders lifted. I jumped to my feet, picked him up and clasped him to my chest, as he continued to howl.

" 'You're okay,' I soothed, rocking him gently. Still shaken, I checked his airway for obstructions. And he did seem fine, just scared.

"When I finally looked around, the shadow was gone, and everything was back to normal.

"Only later did it hit me how close I came to losing him, and I burst into tears.

"Like many new mothers who lack sleep, I lived in a zombie-like state. At the time I believed I'd imagined the dark shadow and the blinding flash of light, so I didn't say anything about the incident to Mort. But I now know this was the first in a series of very odd happenings."

I reread this page several times, not believing what I'm seeing. Of course I don't remember the event she's talking about, but invisible hands holding her to the floor? Really? And "this was the first in a series of very odd happenings."

I have to read on.

"C'mon, break's over." Cassie pounds on the door. "I'm gonna tell Mom she should pay me more than you, if you don't get out of there and come downstairs to help."

"Yeah, yeah," I growl.

I glance at the next page, dated the year I turned nine. Carefully refolding the notes, I stuff them back into my jeans and look in the mirror to make sure they don't show above the pocket.

I flush the toilet and run water, so Cassie will think I was here for another reason.

When I unlock the door and open it, Cassie stands on the other side, towering over me, one hand on her hip. I slug her arm as I pass.

"Ow!"

€ € €

By late afternoon, we've gone through most of the boxes. Only a small pile remains.

I grab a flashlight and head to the last stack, which is in a dark corner, while Cassie works on a box over by the couch.

I shiver. It's seems colder in this part of the basement.

Flicking on my flashlight, I stick the unlit end into my mouth, so I can use both hands to remove the top box. When I lift it, the flashlight reveals a huge nest of spiders underneath. By the dozens, they climb down the sides of the stacked boxes. Some jump to the cement floor.

I drop the box and scoot back – fast.

Suddenly, this corner of the basement seems even darker. A flicker of something black, like a shadow, swirls behind the boxes.

The spiders surge toward me. I aim the beam from my mouthed flashlight at them, and they pause. My light reveals their round bodies. They look like black widows, loads of them!

Gasping, I drop the flashlight. It clanks on the smooth cement and spins like a top.

I want to run, but I'm frozen in place, my skin cold and crawling.

The spiders veer around the fallen flashlight, now aimed at the boxes, to scurry toward me.

Before I can react, they scuttle over my shoes and climb up my jeans. I can't breathe. I can't call for help. I can't get my feet or voice to work.

Something prickly crawls across my belly. I pull up my shirttail and see a spider. Its pinch tells me I've been bitten. Somehow, with trembling fingers, I manage to flick it off.

The spider lands upside down on the floor in the flashlight's beam. The red hourglass shape on its stomach means I was right – they *are* black widows! And I'm gonna die if more of them bite me.

"H-h-h-help!"

Cassie looks over. "What's wrong?"

"Sppppiiiders!" I squeak out.

That voice in my head says, *"Drop and roll."*

The thought of hitting the floor where more of them skitter is horrible, but rolling will smash most of the ones already on me and maybe injure a lot of the ones crawling toward me.

I force my stiff knees to bend and lie flat on the cold cement. Hands at my sides, I twist one direction and then the other, bumping over the flashlight again and again.

"What the heck are you doing?!" Cassie comes running from the other side of the basement. She screams and then disappears.

Was she too scared to stick around?

A moment later, she hovers over me, flashlight in one hand, rolled-up newspaper in the other. She swats spiders off my body and stomps those on the floor.

By the beam of both flashlights, I realize we've hardly made a dent in the swarm. And they keep coming.

I struggle to rise, but something prevents me from moving. Even though I strain with everything I've got, I'm pasted to the floor, just like Mom was. I can't even roll anymore.

All I can do is watch. Cassie whips hundreds of spiders with her newspaper, but it's like putting out a fire with a teacup. No way can she win.

"Calen, move!" she yells.

"I c-c-." I can't even get the word out.

My heart beats faster than I thought possible.

I look down at my white T-shirt. Black shapes creep toward my neck and face.

"Mom, help!" Cassie shouts up the stairs. No response. "Mom!" Cassie screams louder.

More pinches on my neck. I've been bitten again, which makes the hair on my arms stand up.

Before all those grasping, barbed legs can reach my chin, I clamp my eyes and mouth shut. I force my trembling hands over my ears. *I can't let them crawl inside my head!*

I remember praying, "Someone, please help! I don't want to die today!" not knowing if anyone heard me or was even listening.

Chapter 2

Side Note: As I write this down, fear and panic overwhelm me. My heart pounds and my hands shake. I drop my journaling pen. The room spins, and I grab the edge of our tiny kitchen table.

Ten minutes later, after what I now recognize as a panic attack subsides, I drink a Coke and eat a banana. Finally, I'm able to continue.

Still in our basement, same day.

On my back with my eyes squeezed shut, a light, brighter than any flashlight, invades my closed lids and makes me cringe.

What now? My heart slams against my ribs as I sift through possibilities. Have the spiders poisoned me? Is this the light people see when they're dying?

Cassie cries out, but I don't know why. A loud clank on the cement floor tells me she too has dropped her flashlight. Some part of her touches my bare arm.

The bright light dims.

Brushing at my neck and face, I don't feel any creepy crawlies. When I open my eyes, I twist my head from side to side and rub my hands up and down my arms. My white T-shirt has no black specks on it, and my arms are clear of bugs.

Beside me, Cassie is on her knees, hands over her face.

The basement seems a little brighter than before. And I don't see a single spider anywhere.

Where'd they all go? Are they hiding somewhere? Or was I dreaming?

I pinch myself hard to make sure I'm awake. "Ow!"

"Calen!" Cassie touches my shoulder. "Are they gone?"

"Yeah, I think so."

"Yikes, that was bright." She blinks rapidly. "Where'd that light come from?"

"I don't know. Freaky, huh?" I wonder if my plea for help had anything to do with our rescue, but I shake off the idea. Why would a god, if there is one, listen to me? I've ignored "a higher power," as Mom calls it, for most of my life.

Cassie's flashlight has rolled a little ways, so she crawls to it and waves its light around. Even though the basement is cold, her face is sweaty, I'm sure from beating bugs like crazy. "I haven't seen spiders act like that before." She wipes a hand across her forehead.

"Yeah." I nod. "Like they were possessed or something. Have you ever seen so many spiders in one place before?"

Cassie shakes her head.

When Dad helped me with a science report last fall, we learned that black widows don't swarm.

I'm tempted to tell Cassie about Mom's notes, to show her how weird things have happened to me before. But I'm afraid to. What would she think if she knew I seem to attract danger? Would she even want me around?

The wooden stairs to the basement creak, and I turn my head. Mom flies down the steps, two at a time, carrying one of our bright camping lanterns. *Why'd she stop to bring a light?*

She jumps to the hard cement from several steps up and swings the lantern around. Its light floods every corner of this basement room.

When she sees us, she runs over. "I heard you yell, Cassie. What happened?"

Cassie lowers her flashlight. "Gobs of spiders attacked Calen just now."

"I think they were black widows, and they bit me." I rub my arms as if spiders still crawl on them.

"I believe you."

At the time I thought it was weird how she was so willing to believe the unbelievable. It made me wonder what other incredible things have happened, making me more determined to read the rest of those pages.

"The spiders came from those boxes over there." Cassie gestures toward the spooky corner.

Mom hurries over to the remaining stack of boxes, waves the lantern around and then sets it on top of the boxes, making that once-dark corner as bright as day. "I don't see any now."

She comes back and stoops down. "Let's have a look, Calen."

Now that my life is no longer in danger, I'm more aware of the spider bites. They're burning and itching like crazy. I rub my finger across one of them, which feels like a huge blister.

"Don't scratch it," Mom cautions. She turns my head from side to side to check out my neck.

Cassie gasps.

How many bites did I get?

"Is that all of them?" Mom asks.

"There's another." I pull up my T-shirt. The bite on my stomach is not only swollen and puffy, but red streaks, like small octopus tentacles, creep toward my heart. I swallow hard.

My sister drops her flashlight into her lap.

Mom says, "I'll get a cold cloth from the bathroom to help reduce the swelling and then drive you to the hospital."

"Hospital? It's not *that* serious." I don't like doctors.

I prop myself up on my elbows to show I'm okay. But my head feels like it's going to explode, and I massage my forehead to ease the pain.

"You may not feel bad now, but you will."

How do moms know this stuff?

She leaves my line of sight, so I try to get up, only to collapse back.

Mom returns with an ice-cold washcloth and puts it on my neck. The bites feel better immediately. I'm going to be okay.

She places my hand on top of the heavenly washcloth. "Hold this." Grabbing one of my arms, she says, "Let's get you upstairs and into the car. We're not waiting for an ambulance to get way out here."

"Do we have to? I feel better – really."

"Hush, Calen. Cassie, I need your help."

My sister grabs my other arm, and they lift me to my feet.

My noodle-like legs threaten to give out, and I almost drop the washcloth.

Now my head really pounds. I groan.

Mom frowns. "What hurts?"

"My head." I close my eyes. I feel like I'm wearing a too-tight helmet.

"I'll give you some aspirin in the car."

Although I nearly collapse a couple times, we finally make it to the top of the stairs without anyone falling. My muscles feel heavy and tight, and Cassie and Mom are huffing and puffing.

Somewhere along the way, I drop the washcloth.

We turn and stumble toward the garage. My legs weak, Cassie and Mom drag me behind them.

When we finally reach the car, they settle me across the back seat. I'm burning up and shivering all at the same time.

Cassie sits in front of me. Fargo, our Huskie, barks from his dog run at the side of the house. He too knows something's wrong.

"It's okay, Fargo," Cassie reassures.

Mom leans in through an open car window. "I'm going to grab my purse and call the hospital to let them know we're coming." She runs into the house.

A spasm shoots through my stomach. I roll to one side, the pain so intense I pull my knees to my chest. I moan.

"What's wrong?" Cassie hovers over the front seat.

I can't answer 'til the spasm stops. "Stomach cramp," I pant.

Six months ago, when I sprained my ankle, the doctor asked about my level of pain. On a scale of one to ten, my ankle was a six. Just now was an eleven. Maybe I *do* need a hospital after all.

My sister jerks back as I sit up. My head spins. A wave of nausea overwhelms me, and I lean my head back against the seat.

By feel, I manage to click my seatbelt closed after three tries.

Mom comes running out of the house, purse over one shoulder, a bottle of water in one hand and car keys in the other. She slides into the driver's seat and rolls up her window. "They're expecting us."

She tosses her purse and the water bottle to Cassie. "The aspirin's in a side pocket. Give him two." To me she adds, "Be sure to wash them down with lots of water."

Mom starts the engine and revs it up.

Cassie hands me the tablets, along with the water. I pop the pills in my mouth and gulp down half the liquid without a breath. I didn't realize I was so thirsty.

Cassie and I tease Mom that sloths move quicker than she drives. But today is different. While she appears calm, she's a speed demon. She squeals out of the driveway and cranks the shifter into Drive.

When we reach the freeway, I'm jarred to and fro as the old Ford veers from lane to lane. We're passing almost every car.

"Mom, slow down!" Cassie urges.

My head pounds even more. I want to lie down again.

The sky rumbles, and rain batters the windshield. Cassie closes her window, and Mom switches the wipers to full speed.

Another wave of nausea hits me. I swallow rapidly to keep from hurling. Undoing my seatbelt, I sprawl across the seat.

Even though we live in the suburbs, away from town, I wish she'd called an ambulance.

Like I'm not there, Mom tells Cassie, "The doctor who answered the phone said he needs to get anti-venom into Calen a.s.a.p., so he doesn't have a worse reaction. He assumed Calen had been bitten only once. When I told him he was bitten at least a dozen times, the doctor was silent. Finally, he muttered, 'Impossible.' And then he added, 'But, if what you're telling me is true, you need to get him here as fast as you can.' "

My stomach cramps are full-blown now, one after another, and beyond painful. Cassie turns and hangs over the seat each time I groan in agony.

Twice I lose parts of my lunch into a plastic grocery bag I find on the floor. So much for the aspirin, and tuna's not good on the way up.

My part of the car smells like puke now, and I'm sweating buckets. At the same time, I shiver like I'm in a freezer.

Cassie leans over the seat to lay her pink sweater over me. "Here, this'll help." She pinches her nose. She must have caught a whiff of my "lunch."

I remember thinking, *I don't need her girly warmth. Doesn't she know I'll probably throw up on it?*

My stomach spasms again and I groan.

Cars honk and tires squeal. Now that she's off the freeway, Mom must be ignoring stop signs and traffic lights. On the side window, the rain continues to fall in sheets.

We slide to a stop. I sit up, letting the embarrassing sweater drop to my jeans. We've arrived at the hospital's covered emergency entrance. Mom runs inside. Steady clicks tell me the car's turn signal is still blinking.

Between attacks of pain, I rest my forehead on the back of the front seat.

My car door swings open, and I bolt upright. A white-coated guy and what seems like an army of people in green surround a rolling table. Mom stands behind them.

This seems like a lot of fuss, as Grandpa would say, for a few spider bites. They must think it's serious.

The white-coated guy sticks his head inside. He smells like disinfectant, which makes me nauseated again.

Closing my mouth, I try to swallow over a tight throat. I don't want to get sick all over him.

"I'm Dr. Gray," he says, leaning in. The sound of rain thrumming on the metal roof over the entrance threatens to drown him out. "I'm not sure I heard your mother right. You were bitten several times by what you think were black widows?"

"Yes," I croak, shivering.

Cassie peers over the seat. "I've never seen so many spiders."

I rest my head on the back seat, so the doctor can look at the bites. Feeling like I'm going to be sick again, I stick my tongue against the back of my throat and breathe through my nose.

From behind the doctor, Mom adds, "He was bitten about forty-five minutes ago. I gave him aspirin, but he threw them up."

I haven't examined my wounds in a mirror yet. But they must look awful because Dr. Gray holds true to his name and turns pale.

"Very odd," he mutters and looks behind him. "Bring that gurney over here! And help me get him out of the car."

To me he says, "Okay, buddy, let's get you inside."

I shove Cassie's sweater to the floor. Two green-suited men take my arms and lift me out of the car. I can't seem to stand straight and feel as limp as wet paper. Two more "greenies" grab my legs.

The doctor steadies the table on wheels, while the others lift me onto it. I'm glad I don't have to climb up.

Someone covers me to my chin with a blanket, yet I feel like frost has entered my bones. I clutch at my chest because I can't get enough air and shiver because I can't get warm.

Once they have me settled, they grab the sides of the table. I catch one last glimpse of Mom and Cassie before the greenies sprint toward the entrance. Tears roll down Mom's cheeks as she blows me a kiss. Cassie looks pale and scared.

We fly through the automatic doors, while overhead, fluorescent lights zoom past like cars on a freeway. I'm dizzy again.

The urge to vomit is too great. "I'm going to be sick," I warn. Someone near me says, "Go ahead. But turn your head, so you don't choke."

I crank my neck to one side and hurl, but no more lunch comes up, just clear, bad-tasting liquid that pools on the blanket.

My breathing becomes shallow and labored. At the same time, I sweat like I'm in hell, sure I'm soaking my clothes and the blanket.

Another spasm hits, and all my muscles, not just my stomach, contract. The pain is overwhelming. I scream, ashamed but unable to keep silent. I wish someone would just knock me out.

I pant like a dog.

"Get him into Pod 3," Dr. Gray commands. "His diaphragm is becoming paralytic. We need to get anti-venom into him stat."

The last things I remember are two simultaneous needles, an icy cold shot in my upper arm and one of those IV things stabbed into my lower arm.

The pain dulls, and my muscles relax. No more spasms. I breathe easier.

Closing my eyes, I give in to whatever joy juice flows through me.

€ € €

Spiders, a whole squadron of them, march toward me like angry soldiers. These monsters are at least seven-feet tall. Their mandibles click and clack menacingly. Rows of shiny unblinking eyes stare at me.

Behind them, I can make out a shadow as tall as a man. The shadow cackles as the spiders horde over me. Sharp stabs of pain shoot through me as they break through my skin.

Another shape, this one super bright and not human-looking, sends a beam of light at the dark shadow, and it disappears. The spiders turn, see the bright glow and skitter away.

But they're not fast enough.

The blinding flash hurtles toward them. When it connects, all of them disappear in puffs of smoke, leaving behind a bunch of burning, itching bites.

I'm sure I must be dreaming. I mean, who's ever heard of seven-foot tall spiders?

Chapter 3

My Private Notes. After Session Three with Dr. Chapman.

When Dr. Chapman read this last section, she pointed out, "Cassie took your word that they were black widows."

Cassie told me later the shrink convinced her they weren't spiders, but some other kind of swarming bug.

The doctor said, "Everyone overreacted, and you were never in any serious danger. Even if you had disturbed a spiders' nest, they wouldn't have been as aggressive as you described." To quote her, "Most would have retreated back into the shadows."

"What about my medical records?"

"As I told you before, the hospital has no record of your admittance. They've never heard of a Dr. Gray, and none of the staff remembers you."

When I asked Cassie about my hospital stay, she said, "My memory's fuzzy." (Yeah, right!).

So I can't prove any of it. Still, I keep handing pages of my journal over to Dr. Chapman. If I'd made all this up, wouldn't my story keep changing? It never has.

Chapman's Journal. June 8, 1991. The Hospital.

Panic floods through every nerve when I wake, and I take deep breaths.

Where am I? Was the spider attack just a bad dream?

I touch my neck. Nope, no such luck. Some kind of bandage covers the places where I was bit, which still itch and burn. While painful, the bites are more bearable. I fold down the blanket to discover I'm wearing a sweat-soaked shirt-like thing that reminds me of a dress. Gross. Someone must have put it on me while I slept. I hope it was one of the guys.

Raising the neck of my shirt, I look at the wound on my stomach. It's covered with a white pad and tape. I lift a corner of tape. The bite has white stuff on it. It doesn't seem as swollen, and the red lines aimed at my heart are fading. Some round disks are stuck to my chest with wires leading from them.

I follow the wires. They're attached to a machine behind me, where steady beeps signal what I think are my heartbeats. I'm still alive.

Across the room, Mom dozes in a chair, her chin on her chest. A curtain in front of my bed prevents me from seeing into the hall. This looks like some kind of hospital room.

I remember wondering how long I've been here.

And then it hits me. My clothes!

Where are my jeans with Mom's notes in them?

I throw back the covers and sit up, disconnecting some disks on my chest. The machine behind me screeches like a siren.

Mom jumps to her feet. "Calen, stay there!" She rushes to my side, but not before my bare feet hit the cold floor. The IV line snaps apart. The room spins, and my head pounds. The annoying alarm doesn't help.

I lean on the mattress.

Mom grabs my arm. "You're not ready to get out of bed!" she shouts above the screaming machine.

Cold air travels down my spine and makes me shiver. Reaching behind, I discover my shirt-dress is open in the rear. And I'm not wearing underwear!

Hoping Mom can't see my butt, I grab both sides of the material to close the gap.

Can this day get any worse?

Feeling the need to pee, I wonder how I'm going to get to the bathroom. That's when I spy a plastic tube emerging from the bottom of my silly dress. Scowling, I follow the tube to a bag on the side of the bed. It's almost full of yellow liquid – urine?

I guess this day can get worse.

Mom gives me a bear hug. "It's great to see you awake, hon," she says into my ear. "You had us really scared." Her voice breaks.

She holds me at arm's length, a big grin on her face. I wobble, and her grin turns to a frown. She grabs me with both hands and yells above the din. "You need to get back into bed!"

I murmur, "Where are my clothes?"

"Huh? What'd you say?"

I repeat the question louder. I'm not really worried about my clothes, but I *am* worried about losing Mom's notes.

"Your stuff's in that closet over there." She points across the room.

I groan inwardly. While I'm desperate to get to my jeans, I'd never make it that far.

Assuming I want to get dressed, she adds, again in my ear so she doesn't have to shout, "But you can't leave yet. The doctor needs to make sure the venom has cleared your system. They're also monitoring your bites for infection."

To steady my vision and lessen the pain in my head, I lean sideways and rest against my pillow. I want to slug the wailing machine behind me.

I'm aware of someone in blue pants standing next to us. This person reaches around me, and the beeping alarm finally stops. I lift my throbbing head to see a woman whose shirt is the same blue color, but with cartoonish zebras all over it. Mouse ears are perched on her spiky black hair, and black whiskers are drawn across her cheeks.

I blink twice to make sure I'm not imagining her.

Hands on hips, she smiles. She's cute when she smiles. "Have you been exploring, Master Calen?" She makes a tsking sound, and her whiskers wiggle.

I lean against the bed, smooth my hair down with one hand and tug at my half-open dress-thing with the other. "Who *are* you?" I ask. "And why are you dressed so weird?"

She grabs her pant legs, smiles and curtsies, dipping her Minnie Mouse ears. "Nancy, your pediatric ICU nurse, at your service. My costume's meant to make young patients feel less afraid."

"Have I met you before?" Mom asks.

"Have you had a child in intensive care before?" Nancy yanks the curtain in front of my bed more fully closed.

"No."

"Then I don't think we could've met." My nurse pulls back my covers.

"Funny. You look familiar."

When my legs shake again, Nancy grabs my shoulders. "Let's get you into bed, Master Calen. Can you swing your leg up?"

I take a deep breath and boost my butt onto the cool sheet, while Nancy and Mom hold onto me. After a couple of tries, I'm able to lift my right leg onto the bed, which makes me huff and puff.

"Be careful of your catheter," Nancy cautions, pointing to the long tube hanging below the bottom of my dress. She raises my left leg, placing it next to my right, and I hang on to my "shirty" dress to keep it down.

She comes around to the other side of the bed. "Help me get these covers over you again."

Rolling to one side, I realize too late I'm probably mooning her. I clutch at the back of the flimsy material and my face grows hotter.

With the covers over me, I roll onto my back, exhausted and panting. I can't believe I'm such a wimp.

Nancy takes my temperature and then holds my wrist with her cool fingers and looks at her watch.

After a few moments, she says, "Good. Though you still have a slight fever, your heart rate is closer to normal. I predict a long and healthy life for you, full of sports and girlfriends. But you need to remain in bed for now." She grins and claps her hands. "You'll be up and around in no time."

Sure, she can be cheery. She's not half-naked.

"Now, let's get your heart monitor reconnected. Somehow…" She winks. "It's come undone." She goes over to the sink, washes her hands and slips on rubber gloves.

Mom watches from the chair.

Nancy pulls the covers down to my waist. I grip the top of them. With her gloved fingers, she warms the round disks that I disconnected from my chest earlier. She loosens the neck of my hospital shirt, reaches inside and attaches the still-cold metal to my skin, counting with each, "And a one... and a two… and a three..."

She's weird, but I like her.

The steady beep, beep of the machine, what Nancy called a heart monitor, resumes.

"Can you lean forward?" Nancy asks. I lift my head and shoulders, which brings on another dizzy spell, while she re-ties the neck of my dress.

I plop my head back onto the pillow and close my eyes, too weary to do anything else.

The squeak of Nancy's shoes on the linoleum means she's moving around the room. She touches my arm near where the needle was inserted.

"What're you doing?" I ask and open my eyes.

She pretends to twist a moustache at the edge of her mouth. "Bwa ha ha. Wouldn't you like to know?"

Yes, definitely weird.

She smiles. "I'm reattaching your IV line."

My eyelids fall closed once more, and I'm almost asleep when her next suggestion snaps them open again. "Now that you're conscious, we can remove your catheter."

Is she going to see my privates?

"And it's going to hurt a little."

Okay, I take it back. I don't like her so much now.

"Can't a male nurse do it?" I plead, sweat forming on my upper lip. I look to Mom, but she stands and thankfully turns around.

"'fraid not." Nurse Nancy lifts my covers and then my dress-thing. "You're stuck with me."

My face burns hot.

Before I can respond, she asks, "Who's your favorite superhero?"

I say "Super..." She pulls on the tube. "M-a-a-a-n!"

I groan, grab the bedding and jerk upright. *Is she pulling my penis off?*

"I've always loved the red cape," she says. "And being able to fly, wouldn't that be something?"

I'm about to slap her hands away when she says, "There, all done. You've earned Superman status for today." She pulls a happy face sticker out of a pocket and sticks it on the back of my hand.

Is this woman for real?

Sweating from head to toe, I fall back onto the pillow and my arms drop to my sides. I shut my eyes. This is officially the worst day of my life, so far.

The toilet flushes and then a faucet runs.

Nancy's shoes squeak across the floor again. "Are you hungry?" she asks.

My stomach growls at the thought of food. I need to pee, but I'm not going to share that fact. "I'm starved, but first I need to take a walk."

Or, as Grandpa would say, when he's trying to be funny, "See a man about a horse."

The nurse readjusts my covers. "Your doctor hasn't authorized you to leave your bed yet."

Mom adds, "Calen, you need to follow the doctor's instructions, so you can get well as fast as possible."

Nurse Nancy is more perceptive than I thought. She puts a hand on my forearm. "Removing catheters often makes patients feel like they need to use the bathroom." She pats my arm. "Trust me, you don't. But when you do, you can use the bedpan."

She points to a stupidly small, funny-shaped bowl on the table beside the bed.

I frown. *Does she expect me to pee in bed? With my mom in the room?*

"But – good news!" She claps and gives a little hop, like I'm a three-year-old. "The doctor should be in shortly. If everything looks good, I'm sure he'll let you get up. Until then, stay right there and rest. I'll bring you a menu, so you can order a yummy breakfast."

I want to object about the walking part, but I know she's right. I don't have enough strength for even a few steps. And the thought of food makes my mouth water, so I decide to focus on breakfast.

Mom asks Nancy, "Can I speak with you outside?"

"Sure." Nancy nods.

I watch them leave and then eye the closet, wishing I had super powers and could levitate those notes over to my bed.

They stop just outside my room. Between the steady beeps of my heart monitor, I have to strain my ears as Mom mutters, "I need your help, Nancy. Nobody but family and medical personnel can be in Calen's room. Okay?"

"ICU rules demand 'family only' anyway," Nancy states. "What's worrying you?"

"Let's just say Calen's safety is of the utmost importance."

"I'll keep him safe," Nancy reassures. "You can count on it."

Huh, what's that all about?

When Mom returns, I'm sitting up. I want to ask her why she feels I need protecting but decide against it. Then she'd know I eavesdropped.

While part of me wants her to stay, part of me thinks, if she leaves, I can ask the nurse to bring me my jeans. "Mom, I'll be fine here. Why don't you go home?"

She comes over to my bed. "I want to hear what the doctor has to say first." Stroking my overgrown hair off my forehead, she adds, "But, after two days, I really do need a shower."

"What?! I've been here two days?"

"Yes, and you were out the entire time. The doctor said, if you hadn't gotten the anti-venom when you did, you wouldn't have made it.

Your lungs were shutting down, and your heart was out of control." Her voice quivers, and she takes a deep breath.

"Have you been here the whole time?"

"Of course."

"Where's Cassie? And Dad?"

"They were here for a long time and left only a little while ago." As if she senses my unspoken guilt trip, she adds, "But none of this is your fault, Calen. Those spiders were…odd." She draws out the last word. "The doctor's never seen so many black widow bites on one person before. He says that's not normal."

And you know more about such weirdness than you're willing to share, right Mom?

I start to ask her what she knows when a thin guy in a white coat strides into my room. He looks familiar, with brown hair and eyes and large-framed glasses. He smiles, showing straight white teeth. "Ah, my favorite patient."

Yeah, right. I've been unconscious this whole time.

I smirk. "I bet you tell *all* your patients that."

He grins. "Maybe."

Mom moves out of the way.

He holds a clipboard in one hand and thrusts his other hand out for a shake. "Do you remember me, Calen? Dr. Gray."

I hadn't remembered his name, but I grab his hand and shake it. "I think so."

He looks at the clipboard and studies the heart monitor. As if I'm not in the room, he says, "His temperature is closer to normal, and his heart has a regular and slower rhythm." He catches my eye. "You gave us quite a scare, young man."

I like it when someone calls me a man. I wish Mom would.

"Good thing you're young and healthy." He smiles. "Others would've succumbed to so much venom in their system."

The doctor puts down the clipboard, snaps on a pair of rubber gloves, grabs a small cloth from a wall dispenser and pulls a tube of something out of a drawer.

"Now let's have a look at those bites."

I lean my head back, and Dr. Gray says, "I'm going to remove the gauze and tape, which might sting." In one yank, he rips the tape up from around my neck wounds.

"Yowch!" I yell. Okay, I'm officially cranky now.

"Sorry, but quicker is better." He wipes the strong-smelling but cooling cloth across my neck. "Ah, these are healing nicely. We'll just squeeze a little more antibiotic cream on them and leave them uncovered." The cream feels even colder than the cloth.

He throws the wipe away and pulls out another. Then he lifts up my shirt and folds it across my chest. I'm grateful he leaves the blanket across my hips. "You know the drill. I apologize in advance. This is going to hurt."

Another yank. I put a hand over my mouth to muffle my cry. Dr. Gray finishes cleaning the wound.

I lift my head. Around the bite is a red ring. Inside the ring, the skin has been eaten away.

The doctor nods. "This one's getting a lot better too."

Really? It looks gross to me.

He rubs more cream over it and replaces the gauze with a new pad, which he surrounds with adhesive tape. "We'll keep this one covered a while longer, since your hospital gown rubs against it."

What an appropriate name. A "gown." Chosen by a female, I'm sure.

He rubs his chin. "Because yours is a most unusual case, do you mind if I ask you a few questions?"

I sit up straighter, trying to look more energetic than I feel, so he'll let me out of this bed. "Shoot."

"Tell me how you disturbed the spider nest."

"I pulled the top box off a stack in our basement, and dozens of them came crawling out." I shudder at the memory.

When the doctor finishes writing, he asks, "Was there anything unusual about the spiders? Did they look like normal black widows?"

"Yeah, but they didn't act like normal spiders, at least not the black widows I've read about."

"You're right." Dr. Gray nods. "Black widows are quite solitary."

His next statement surprises me. "I'd like to write an article about your experience."

I'm not sure I want my friends reading such a thing. What will they think? That I'm some kind of spider magnet? Or will they think I'm brave?

"Who's going to read it?"

"Just some doctors who treat venomous bites. You won't see it on the evening news or in the papers. No pictures of your face." He smiles and pats my arm. "Okay?"

"I guess." *But I feel like some kind of experiment.*

He pushes his glasses higher on his nose. "How did you feel after getting so many bites?"

"Lousy."

He chuckles. "Can you be more specific? Maybe use a simile, you know, 'like or as?' "

I know what a simile is.

He pulls a pad from his pocket. "I'll be taking notes."

I sigh. "They itched, like the worst case of chicken pox on the planet. While the rest of my body was on fire, my neck seemed covered in ice cubes.... And then the cramps... the nastiest I've ever felt, like my organs were in a vise.... And then came full-body spasms, making my muscles as hard as concrete. All the time, I had trouble catching my breath, like I'd just run a sprint."

Is that enough similes for you?

"Excellent. How long did those full-blown symptoms take to manifest? Sorry, I mean how long did it take for the body spasms to start?"

Duh, I read the dictionary. In my head I quote, *"Manifest – to display or demonstrate by one's actions or appearance."*

"Maybe half an hour or so?" I tilt my head and look at Mom. She nods.

"Amazing. If your mom hadn't gotten here when she did ... Well, let's just say, you're one lucky guy."

"Thanks, Mom. I'm glad you drove so fast."

"Uh, yeah..." She clears her throat. "I'm just grateful you're okay."

"When can I get up?" I ask the doctor.

"Venom takes time to leave your body, even with the multiple doses of anti-venom I gave you. But you should be back to normal very soon. In the meantime, until your strength returns, I'll place an order for a physical therapist to help you, with a walker."

I stare at him. *A walker? What am I? Eighty?*

I'm itching to read those notes before something more horrible happens, so I ask, "If I can't get up, can I at least put my clothes on?"

"With your catheter out, you can wear underwear. Let's stick with the gown a while longer."

I sigh. *Better than being butt-naked, I guess.*

Dr. Gray turns to my mom. "Do you have any questions, Mrs.

Ambrose?"

"When can he go home?"

"I want to keep an eye on him for at least another 48 hours, to make sure those bites heal well. At such time as he can get up on his own and take a shower, I'll discharge him."

"Thanks." She smiles. "Great news, right Calen?"

I shrug. *Better news would be if I could go home right now.*

Still looking at my mom, the doctor adds, "He's going to be fine. But you look like you could use a good night's sleep."

"You're right." She yawns. "I'll have his dad come sit with him."

"You and Dad don't have to hang around. I'll probably just eat and sleep most of the time. Maybe watch a little TV." I look up at the blank screen in a corner of the room. "You'd be bored stiff." *Translation: I don't need a babysitter.*

"Calen, it's all part of being a parent. Someday you'll understand." To Dr. Gray, she says, "Thank you, Doctor. We appreciate all you've done."

She looks at me and nods her head toward the doctor.

I get the message. "Yes, thank you," I add.

"You're quite welcome." He gives me a pat on my head, which makes me want to slug him, and says, "I know it's hard just to lie in bed, but it's the best thing you can do. Your body's been through a major trauma."

I remember thinking, *If you say so. But first chance I get, I'm going to prove I'm ready to go home.*

After the doctor leaves, Mom gathers up her purse and keys. She comes over to the bed and gives me a kiss on the forehead. "See you later, hon, and enjoy your breakfast. Don't worry. Your dad will be here in a little while. I love you."

"Love you too, Mom."

At the curtain, she waves before disappearing behind it.

I close my eyes. *Now, how am I going to get to my clothes?*

Within a few moments, Nurse Nancy peeks around the curtain in front of my bed. She holds up a clipboard. "Here's your breakfast menu." She shows me how to elevate my bed to a sitting position, so I can mark what I want to eat. She waits while I decide.

My hunger demands I choose everything on the menu. But the memory of upchucking a tuna sandwich is still fresh in my mind, so I take it slow. I check eggs, bacon, French toast, orange juice and milk.

She looks at the clipboard. "Are you done?"

"Yep."

"Great, I'll send this down to the cafeteria." She reaches for the clipboard.

"Wait." I put up a hand. "I need a favor."

"Okay. " She tilts her head. "What?"

"I left something important in my jeans, and the doctor says I can wear underwear now. Can you bring them both to me?" Normally, I'd be too embarrassed to talk about my underwear to a female, but Nancy's already seen more of me than almost anyone.

She smiles. "Be glad to." After searching the closet, she retrieves my jeans and briefs.

When she hands them to me, she says, "I'll let you change in private."

After she pulls the curtain closed and leaves, I throw back my blankets, pull on my underwear, which leaves me breathless, and check the back pocket of the jeans. Empty.

I search all the pockets again and again, but they're all empty! My heart pounds, and the monitor behind me beeps faster.

Nancy runs in. "Your heart's racing again." She stares at the monitor and then pulls my blankets over me again. "Are you feeling all right?"

"I hope I didn't lose something important. Could you check the bottom of the closet for me when you put my jeans back?"

"Glad to. What should I look for?"

"A bunch of folded note paper."

She opens the closet door again. "I saw those papers," she states. "They fell out of your jeans. I stuffed them into one of your shoes, along with the watch you were wearing."

I'd forgotten about Dad's old watch. I'm glad it's still there.

"Are they important?" she asks.

"Yeah." *Only the most important information of my life.*

Sticking her head into the closet, she bends over. When she straightens up, she has Mom's notes in her hand. "Voila!" she exclaims.

"That's great, Nancy!" Worried she might have gotten curious, I ask, "Did you read them?"

"No. I could get in a lot of trouble for that." She closes the closet door, walks over to my bed and hands me the notes. "Now, I'd better get your breakfast order in before it's too late." She picks up the clipboard.

"One more thing. Who took off my clothes?"

"Two other nurses changed you into your hospital gown and cleaned you up."

I shake my head. *Two women saw me naked? Cleaned me up? Gross. I can't think about that right now.*

"Okay, thanks."

Suddenly tired, I close my eyes. I'll read more of Mom's notes after a little nap.

Chapter 4

My Private Notes. After Session Four with Dr. Chapman.

At our last session, after Dr. Chapman read about my hospital stay, she looked over her glasses at me. "You certainly have a vivid imagination, young man." Like I made it all up.

I pointed to where the spiders attacked my neck. "What about these?"

She leaned forward to examine my bites. "Nothing unusual there."

She's right. When I studied those wounds in a mirror, the skin looked almost normal. Odd. My neck should have really ugly scars on it.

I lifted my shirt to show her the bite on my abdomen. "What about that?" I pointed to the small white mark on my skin.

"That could have been caused by anything, even a slide into home base." She smiled.

I groaned in frustration.

Cassie already told me she isn't going to confirm what happened, which is silly. She fought those dang spiders as hard as I did. But I understand her reasons. We have no evidence they were black widows or that I was hospitalized. And this doctor isn't going to believe a word either of us says, without someone from the hospital backing us up. Which makes me really mad.

And then I remembered there *was* proof somewhere. I told the shrink, "My doctor was going to write an article about my experience in some medical magazine. Is there a way to find it?"

Dr. Chapman shook her head. "I've searched the AMA archives and several other medical journals. I'm sorry. No such article was ever written."

I slammed a fist on the chair arm.

"But I still want you to write down your experiences. Your journal is helping me help you."

I bit my tongue so I wouldn't cuss at her.

Chapman's Journal. Still June 8, 1991. The Hospital.

High up in the corner, a dark shadow sends a pitch-black finger snaking toward me. I can't move and wonder what it'll feel like. *Cold? Sharp? Slimy?*

Will it suck the life out of me?

When the shadow touches me, it feels like human skin, which freaks me out, and I yell.

"Calen, it's me. Nancy." I open my eyes and sigh with relief.

Nancy looks worried. "Sorry to disturb you. I didn't want your breakfast getting cold."

My heart monitor goes crazy.

"Bad dream?" she asks.

I nod.

"You'll feel better after a good breakfast." She reaches up to the heart monitor, and the beeping stops, then goes back to a normal rhythm.

Pushing the button to elevate my head, I wipe sweat from my forehead and scoot up.

A tray rests on the table by my bed. Rolling it toward me, Nurse Nancy removes a metal cover to reveal a steaming, delicious-smelling plate of French toast, eggs and bacon.

"Dig in!" She grins.

I salivate like a Pavlov dog. I know I'm not supposed to hear about Pavlov 'til college, but Dad mentioned him a while ago. When I asked for more info, he loaned me a book about Pavlov's experiments. Really interesting stuff.

Nancy checks my IV drip one more time, then leaves me to wolf down my breakfast. When Dad was in the hospital last year, he said the food was gross, but everything on my plate tastes great. Of course, I gobble it down so fast that I don't taste much of it.

I decide it's really good to be alive, even if I am stuck in this bed for a while.

Nancy returns as I'm enjoying the last bite.

"Would you like a sponge bath?" She pulls away the table on wheels.

"No way!" The thought of my cute nurse seeing all of me again makes my ears burn hot. I cross my arms over my chest. "I'll wait 'til I can take a shower."

Nancy rolls her eyes. She goes over to a bank of drawers across the room, opens one and pulls out something. She hands me a black stick. "Here's the TV remote. We have lots of channels."

"Thanks." I push the red power button and lower the head of my bed a little.

Dad peers around the curtain at the foot of my bed. "Hi, Son."

"Hi, Dad." I smile and turn off the TV.

Dressed in his usual summer teaching clothes—slacks, shirt and bow tie—he comes over and squeezes my shoulder. "You had us all worried there for a while."

Nancy reaches out her hand. "Hi, I'm Nancy."

Hello. Mort." He shakes her offered hand across my bed, one hand still behind him.

"How's our patient?" Dad asks, pushing up his eyeglasses.

"Doing quite well." She looks down at me. "Chomping at the bit to get out of bed. We're waiting on the delivery of a walker to help his balance." She pats my arm. "Anything else you need?"

I shake my head.

"I'll check back on you later." She grins at me and wiggles her nose, reminding me of a mouse.

She looks at Dad. "Nice meeting you."

"Same here." Dad nods.

She scurries away, her tiny feet seeming to float above the ground.

Dad sits on the end of my bed. "I thought you'd enjoy a change from hospital food." He pulls a brown paper bag from behind his back.

Inside are a burger and fries from Charlie's, my favorite fast-food place.

"Wow, Dad, this is swell!" I unwrap the burger and take a deep whiff of mustard, pickles and grilled meat, before taking a big bite. Even though I just finished breakfast, I always have room for a burger.

Dad scoots a little closer. "How are you? Really."

"Okay," I say around a mouthful of burger. "Just having a few bad dreams."

"Understandable, but you don't have to worry about spiders attacking you again. I had the basement fumigated."

I want to say, "That won't help, Dad. Those were abnormal spiders, possessed by some kind of dark force." But I know he'd never believe me. And why should he? I hardly believe it myself.

And what if I told him about the dark shadow, the likely source of the spiders, hovering behind the boxes? Would he think I'm crazy?

Instead, I say, "Thanks," and pop a French fry into my mouth.

"Cassie is anxious to see you. She says she'll stop by later, after class."

Because my sister was so sick from strep throat last spring, she's taking summer school twice a week.

He leans forward. "Grandpa's coming too. He wants to see how you're doing and show you his new watch. I told him you'd be interested."

With my mouth full of burger, I just nod.

Ever since I got Dad's old one running again, watches are my new fascination. Mom also let me take apart a broken clock she was going to throw away. I cleaned it and got it working again. Now it sits on our mantel, reminding me I'm good at fixing mechanical things.

Dad's telling me about a student of his who changes his hair color every week, from blue to purple to bright red, when Grandpa Ambrose strolls into my room.

I wrap up my half-eaten burger.

When I was little, I couldn't say Grandpa, so I called him G. I have ever since.

He removes his ball cap, revealing a bald head, and tips it toward me like a salute. "Looking much better, Grandson." He smiles, which causes his graying handlebar moustache to twitch. "I was worried there for a while, but you're a real trooper. Brought you the latest issues of *Popular Mechanics*." He plops the stack of my favorite magazines on the rolling table. Then he settles into the chair.

"Cool, G." I seem to do more things with my grandpa than my dad, but G's retired and has lots of free time. Dad, on the other hand, works long hours as a professor and even teaches classes in the summer. Despite his work, he makes time to come to almost all my baseball games.

This summer, G and I have gone to the zoo, the county fair, several car shows and a robotics convention, the highlight of my year. He believes sometime in the future, maybe within my lifetime, robots will be building things for us, cleaning our houses and cooking our meals. Sounds like fantasy to me, along with fairies and dragons. But who knows? People thought Da Vinci and Verne were silly dreamers and look at how many of their ideas became reality.

Of course, dark shadows hovering in corners and spiders attacking for no reason used to be fantasy too. Maybe they still are.

"Dad said you got a new watch. Can I see it?"

"Sure." G rises from the chair and thrusts out his wrist. It has a gold-colored band and a square face, like a miniature TV monitor. The face flashes 10:40 a.m. Numbered buttons from zero to nine sit below the display.

"It's something brand new called 'digital' with a calculator built in," he says. "Watch this."

G types in some numbers, pushes a button on the side and says, "Forty-eight divided by four is: Voila! Twelve." G shows me the watch face, which flashes a twelve.

"Wow."

"I can also find out what time it is in Beijing." He pushes another button on the side. "It's 12:40 a.m. there – tomorrow." He turns his wrist, and the watch face does in fact display the date and time for Beijing.

"Let me see." Dad leans over to look. "How much did that set you back?"

"A couple hundred."

Unlike most people his age, G loves new technology. I guess that's why he's so much fun to be around.

"What about your old watch?" I ask.

"Still works, but it's passé now. Gotta keep up with the times." He twirls the end of his moustache and chuckles. "Pun intended."

I groan. "Can I have it, your old watch I mean?" I want to take it apart because it's Swiss-made and expensive. Maybe I can figure out what makes that kind of watch run better and longer than others.

"Sure. I'll bring it along next time I visit." His eyes narrow. "Would you like me to bring your tools too?" Dad gifted me with a set of jeweler's tools and a flask of oil last Christmas. Since then, I've used them a lot.

I grin. G's figured out what I plan to do to his watch. "That'd be great." After all, I can view just so much TV without my brain melting.

Cassie peeks around the curtain and then runs over to me. "Calen!" she squeals. She drops her backpack to the floor and leans over to grab me in a big hug. "I'm so glad you're awake!"

"Okay, okay. Let me breathe." I try to push her away.

Her actions surprise me. Was I really so close to dying? I thought everybody was exaggerating, but maybe not.

Nancy follows Cassie into the room. "Only two visitors at a time in the ICU. I'm sorry, but one of you will have to leave."

Before the others can respond, Cassie says, "I can stay with Calen. I'm done with school for the day, and I brought my homework." She points to the pack. "Besides, we've got a lot to catch up on."

"Well, I *do* have papers to grade." Dad rubs his chin. "I can come back tonight."

"And I have a doctor's appointment..." G looks at his watch. "Soon. Nothing to worry about. But I'll bring you my old watch and your tools afterward." He rises from the chair and heads for the hall, stopping by my bed. "See you later, sport." He squeezes my arm.

"Sounds good."

"Then it's settled." Cassie picks up her bag and tosses it into the now-vacated chair.

Dad rises from my bed and gives me a rare kiss on my forehead. *Yup, I must've been really sick.*

G turns and waves goodbye before he disappears around the curtain. Dad and Nancy follow.

My sister unzips her pack and rummages through it to remove her algebra book and some paper. She looks over at me. "You look tired."

"I am, but it's weird. All I've done in the past two days is sleep."

"Sleep is good." Grabbing her bag from the chair, she plops into the seat and puts her bag on the floor. "I've got a ton of homework. We'll talk more after you nap."

Cassie opens her book and wets the tip of her pencil with her tongue as she begins to write.

I close my eyes but snap them open at the sound of metal sliding against metal. Nancy has pushed back the curtain halfway. She strides into my room.

"Great news! Your Uncle George is here. He heard about your attack, and he's anxious to see you."

"Uncle George? I don't have an Uncle George." Mom's caution to Nancy about visitors comes to mind. "Whoever he is, Nancy, he's not family."

I shiver. Suddenly, the room has gotten much colder.

A red light pulses beyond the curtain. Nancy whips around, a stick now in her hand.

A wand?

She sets her feet next to my bed and raises the stick.

Chapter 5

Like some medieval monk, a hooded and robed figure also holding a stick in his hand glides past the curtain and stops. Unlike the basement shadow, this threat's solid. My heart thunders against my ribs, and the monitor behind me beeps wildly.

"How'd you get past the nurses' station? You're not Calen's Uncle George." Nancy's eyes tighten.

From deep inside the hood, a male voice answers. "I can appear as dumpy Uncle George or whoever I choose. And your nurses are all taking naps." He snorts under his breath. "I find this costume adds an intimidation factor."

Nancy stomps her foot. "You don't belong here. Leave! NOW!"

"I don't think so. I only just got here and the fun has yet to begin." He points his stick at me.

Cassie hops up from her chair, her math book and papers flying to the floor. "She's right. Get out of here!" She stomps forward, gripping her quivering pencil like a dagger.

The monk directs his stick at her and mutters "Sedeo." He must be wielding a magic wand because unseen hands seem to shove her back into the chair. "Nooo!" she screams. She reaches down, picks up her book and holds in front of her like a shield.

"This is not your fight." His voice is low and menacing. "I only want the boy. He should never have been born."

I throw back my covers and lean forward. Panic floods through me.

What can I do to keep him from hurting me, or anyone else?

I grab the closest thing I can find as a weapon – the remote.

Nancy stands closer to me. A red lightning bolt shoots out of the monk's wand with a snap and the smell of rotten eggs.

I twist away, ready to feel the heat and pain of his shot. When I don't, I turn back. Nancy has snagged the bolt with her wand before it could reach me. "I will *not* let you hurt him!"

She flicks her wand at the monk, and his captured bolt zings back through the air at him. He ducks, but the shot catches his arm. He jolts back.

Distracted by Nancy, he doesn't see me throw the remote. It smacks him in the head.

"Fire and brimstone!" he hollers, grabbing his head. He staggers but regains his footing and aims his wand at me. Snap! Another bolt zigzags from his wand.

I close my eyes, helpless to do anything but watch. I figure I'm dead.

When I open my eyes, Nancy has again intercepted his shot and sent it back. She twirls and twirls her wand and then points it at him. A stream of jagged purple bolts bombard the monk, one after the other, their swift snaps sounding like the cracks of a whip. Smoke fills the air, as well as the stinging smell of something like gunpowder.

My attacker deflects the volley, the sizzling blows ricocheting off his wand. He fights back with rapid fire of his own, but Nancy is too fast for him. She refracts each of his searing attacks, 'til one misses her wand. She stoops, and it flies over her head, careening toward Cassie, who's still in the chair.

"Watch out!" I yell.

Still stuck in the chair, she ducks. "How dare you!" She throws her algebra book at the monk.

With a flourish of his wand, he pulverizes it and snickers.

"That was school property!" Cassie wails. She puts her hands on her hips.

Nancy thrusts more purple blows his way, but he conjures a clear shield around himself that stops the bolts from reaching him.

When Nancy momentarily lowers her wand, the shield disappears. Stretching out, the monk begins a steady barrage of crackling red bolts. Nancy successfully defends them all, except one that bounces off her wand and catches her in the shoulder. Her wand drops to the floor, and she grabs her arm.

He swirls his stick and arcs a bolt at her stomach. She crumples on the floor near my bed.

"Nancy!" I cry. I look at the monk and growl. I wish I had a baseball or a bat right now. I'd make him wish he hadn't done that.

He slowly turns in my direction. Like a villain in some melodrama, he mutters, "Heh, heh."

My heart thrums in my ears. *Is this for real?*

Because of his hood, I can't see his features, but I imagine them contorting into an evil grin as he approaches, step by step. Shivers run up my spine. My palms feel wet. "Somebody, I need help!"

Cassie yells, "Leave him alone!" She can stand now, so she slinks forward, scowl on her face, pencil pointed at him.

"Cassie, don't!" *Like her pencil is a match for his wand.*

Zap! Blue sparks shoot over my bed to strike Cassie in the chest. She freezes in place, looking as scared as I feel, her pencil poised in mid-air.

"Stop!" I flip to my knees, fists held high, shaking with anger and fear. "Leave everyone else alone. It's me you want." *If I can get in just one surprise punch.*

The monk is so close now I can smell his rotten breath. "At last. You're mine." He chortles.

With his face in shadow, all I can see is the tip of a beak-like nose. I'll aim for it.

I draw back a fist.

He stretches forward, the long, broad sleeve of his wand-arm hanging down, his wand directed at my chest.

Side Note: I have another panic attack as I remember how I felt that day and have to lay down my pen. After resting for a few minutes, I'm able to continue writing.

Back to the Hospital.

"Immobilis," the monk says.

I can't move, and my clenched fist hangs in the air.

He swirls his stick and mutters under his breath. Black sparks form on the wand's tip.

I'm dead meat.

Not sure if anyone is listening, I shoot a silent plea upward. I don't want to die!

A brilliant throbbing light blinds me, I assume from his wand. I close my eyes.

This must be it, my last breath.

I wait to feel the pain of the monk's blast, but don't feel anything. *Am I dead?*

Another voice, not the monk's, snaps, "No you don't!" A moment passes before I hear, "Oblittero."

Behind my closed lids, the light fades. I open my eyes. Everything has gone black and silent.

I remember thinking how I must be in some kind of black void. *The afterlife?*

For a few heartbeats, I don't move, waiting to see what's next. Someone mumbles, but I don't understand the unfamiliar words.

Finally, I inhale deeply, realizing I've forgotten to breathe for a few seconds.

Suddenly the light returns, and I'm lying back in bed with the blanket over me. *How can that be?*

Cassie sits in the chair, her algebra book open on her lap, her paper on top. She's writing out her homework like before. Her book is intact, as is her homework. *Weird.*

I grab for Mom's notes under my covers, relieved to find them still there. "What just happened?"

Cassie looks up, her eyes glassy. "What do you mean? Everything is fine. It's all fine."

"Didn't you get zapped, you know, frozen?"

"Zapped? Frozen?" She giggles. "You must be on some good pain medicine."

But the dream was so real. I look down, glad to discover Nancy is no longer on the floor.

I lean over to peer around the curtain but can't see anything. Everything out there seems quiet.

I push my call button but don't get a response. *Where's Nancy, or one of the other nurses? Are they still sleeping from the monk's spell?*

Minutes pass. Nothing else attacks me, so I shake off the experience as an odd dream. Maybe Cassie's right. The drugs are making me imagine stuff.

Once I've stopped trembling and realize Cassie is concentrating hard on her algebra homework, I pull out the second page of Mom's notes from under my covers. Maybe they will have clues to explain the strangeness that's become my life.

My mom begins:

July 5, 1987. (I was nine.)

> *"Calen went fishing with his Grandpa Ambrose."*

The curtain in front of my bed rustles. I stuff the page under my pillow just as Nancy strolls in with a clipboard.

"You pressed your button. Did you need something?"

I take a good long look at her. She appears unhurt. "Not really. Just thought everyone had left for the day because it was so quiet out there."

"We're all fine. Everything's fine." Nancy mimics Cassie's tone of voice, like some pre-rehearsed script.

She plops the clipboard on my bed table and does an extended hop, as if she's wearing wings. "Double good news! It's lunchtime and you're being transferred upstairs to the pediatric floor. A walker will be sent up there, along with a physical therapist. You'll be up and around in no time."

"Terrific!" They're finally letting me out of bed. I can pee in a toilet again. Finding her happiness contagious, I smile big.

"And the even better news is – wait for it – I'm transferring with you." She bows.

"You are? How come?" Not that I object. If I'm stuck in this hospital, it's nice to have a cute girl to look at.

She smiles. "I put in for a transfer to the pediatric ward weeks ago. I wanted a change."

Something bugs me. Nancy claims she asked for the transfer weeks ago. But the timing seems awfully convenient. Like maybe she wants to keep an eye on me.

Part of me doesn't believe the strange Uncle George experience was a dream either. My dreams are never that real, and everybody's acting so strange.

So I test her by saying, "I'm glad you're okay."

"Of course I'm okay. Why wouldn't I be?" She raises her eyebrows, which causes her mouse ears to quiver.

Still not willing to accept the recent strangeness as a vision, I ask, while I fill out my lunch request, "What about Uncle George?"

"Who?" She frowns.

"You know. The guy who said he was anxious to see me. I told you he wasn't family."

She tilts her head. "The only people who have been to see you are your mom, your dad, your grandpa and your sister. Nobody named George."

Cassie looks up from her homework. "Calen, we don't have an Uncle George." She addresses Nancy. "He's been talking weird ever since he woke up."

Nancy makes another tsking noise. "I'll ask the doctor about changing your meds. I heard you yelling in your sleep, and now it seems you're having hallucinations." She winks.

€ € €

My new room on the pediatric floor is bigger and doesn't smell strongly of antiseptic. When I uncover my waiting lunch – milk, a ham and cheese sandwich, a banana and a brownie—my stomach growls.

"Wow," Cassie says, "look at that view." I follow her gaze out the fourth-story window and watch the sunshine spotlight the tree-covered mountains.

I really don't want to share my lunch, but I tell Cassie, "You can have half my sandwich."

"Thanks, bro, but I've got a sack lunch."

When we've both finished our meals, Cassie gives me the big-sister spiel before she leaves. "Take care of yourself and get some rest. Mom will be back soon."

Finally alone, I'm able to read more of Mom's notes, which I hid in my underwear when they moved me from the ICU.

Still July 5, 1987.

"Calen and his Grandpa Harley camped in the Allegheny National Forest and fished for most of the first day.

"The second day, Harley tells me, they hiked up a steep trail along the edge of a tree-lined cliff with Calen in front.

" 'All was going fine,' Harley said, 'until Calen fell over the cliff's edge.'

"He added, 'Thank God for the small outcropping of rock that broke his fall, or he'd have been killed. He lay there while I got some rope from my truck and pulled him to safety. I'm grateful he only had scrapes and bruises to show for it. Nothing broken.'

"When I pressed Calen's grandpa for how he fell, he warned, 'You won't believe me.'

" 'Try me.'

"He sighed. 'Calen appeared to be shoved by an unseen force. He didn't stumble, and I didn't bump into him. He tipped sideways, even though it was a windless day.'

" 'He righted himself, but then received what looked like another, harder push and over the edge he went.'" He shook his head. "I grabbed for him, but couldn't reach him in time.'

" 'I know what I'm saying sounds crazy.'

"How could I tell him he wasn't crazy? How could I explain that my son is afflicted by evil, something that's not a part of our material *world? Instead I reassured him with, 'It's not your fault. I'm grateful you were there for him.'*

"I didn't tell him about the other weird accidents Calen survived. Like when he was two and we went to the local swimming pool. I was getting ready to put on his water wings when suddenly he was jerked away, suspended momentarily in the air and then dropped into the pool. Some nice lady with spiky black hair grabbed him and kept his head above water, until I could get to him."

I'm glad my heart monitor isn't attached anymore because my heart races and a sick feeling settles into my chest.

Why is my life in danger so often? …Am I cursed? I read a book once about a kid who was cursed, but it was fiction.

And who's behind all this? The robed figure may not be the only one after me. Is some malevolent spirit out to get me? Or is God paying me back for not giving him the attention he deserves?

While I don't believe in ghosts or God, most of the time anyway, how else can I explain the invisible forces that threw me into a pool and pushed me over a cliff?

And what about the black-haired lady at the pool who saved me? Could that have been Nancy, watching out for me even back then?

I'm glad to finally learn where my phobia of cliffs started. I can't walk near a cliff's edge without getting dizzy and nauseous. And I'm not a fan of water either.

I have to stuff the notes under my pillow again because the physical therapist, a buff guy in blue, shows up with a walker.

He introduces himself as John.

I slowly get to my feet on shaky legs, and John rolls the walker over to me.

"Don't set any speed records, okay?" He grins.

"Very funny."

John and I spend half an hour strolling around the pediatric floor using my walker. One hand grips the walker and the other keeps the gap in my gown closed. I peek in at the other kids. A few have legs in casts, elevated above them, which makes me grateful to be up and around.

I have to stop and lean on the walker or a wall from time to time. John says that's normal after what I've been through. He says my strength and balance will soon return. Hard to believe I was playing baseball for hours at a time just a week ago.

When we get back to my room, John adds, "You did great for your first time out."

"If you say so." I yawn. "I feel like I need another nap."

"Go for it," he adds, as he helps me back into bed.

I'd love to read some more of Mom's notes, but I'm too tired. So I drift off as the hospital PA system calls for some doctor named "Bennett."

Next thing I know, Nancy is checking my pulse. "Hi sleepyhead. How do you feel?" She's placed another clipboard on my table.

"Better. Could I try to make it to the bathroom, with my walker of course?"

"Sure." She nods. "I'll stick around to make sure you get there – safe and sound."

I must look nervous because she grins. "Don't worry. I won't stay by your side the whole time."

"Thanks."

My walker creaks as I roll into the bathroom. I'm surprised by how sore my arms and legs are from the little bit of exercise I got today.

I close the wide door behind me.

Nancy calls, "Holler if you need me." *As if.*

When I finish, I open the door and lean on the walker. Accompanied by the squeak of its wheels on the smooth floor, I creep like a tortoise back to bed.

Nancy helps me crawl into bed and tugs the covers over my legs.

I notice something sticking out of her pocket. It looks like the tip of the wand she used in my so-called dream.

"What's that?" I ask, pointing to her pocket.

My Private Notes.

After reading the above, Dr. Chapman looked over her glasses again and said, "Have you accepted that your hospital stay and the attack were hallucinations?"

I nodded, even though I still had my doubts. She might be right about the attack. No one else remembered it, not Nancy, not Cassie. But I *know* I was in the hospital.

"Dreams can seem very real," Dr. C explained. "To make irrational events seem logical, our minds try to fill in the gaps for things we don't know or understand."

I wanted to say, "My imagination is good, but not that good." Besides, I've never been in an Intensive Care Unit before, so how was I able to explain how it all works? How did I know about the two-person rule, the IV, the catheter, the heart monitor?

Instead I remained silent and nodded my head. I hoped the therapy would be over soon.

She then asked, "Do you read a lot of fantasy?"

While I felt this was a cheap shot, I had to confess I do.

Chapter 6

Chapman's Journal. Still June 8, 1991. The Hospital.

Nancy turns away and mumbles something. Then she whirls around. In her hand is a wooden stick with metal pieces stuck into slots in the wood.

"Can I see that?"

She hands me the unique-looking object. "It's a tambourine stick."

"Oh, yeah." I turn it over in my hand. "I used to play one of these in grade school."

"I use it to distract younger patients when I have to remove a catheter, give a shot or put in an IV."

I shake the wood, and it makes a tinkling sound. "Neat." But it's not what I saw poking out of her pocket a minute ago. That stick was thinner and darker.

"Do you have anything else in there?" I stare at her pocket.

She pulls open the blue, zebra-covered material to reveal an empty space.

When I look up, I catch the briefest smirk on her face before she breaks into a smile and points at the clipboard. "Fill out your menus. You have enough meals there for two days. The doctor doesn't think you'll be here longer than that." She thumbs her nose. "You're breaking out of this joint."

"Yessss." I smile and pump my fist.

"Oh, and some of your baseball buddies are here to see you." She takes the tambourine stick and puts it in her pocket. "Should I send them in?"

"In a minute." Worried about bed head, I smooth my hair with my hands and swipe a fist across my mouth, in case any of my lunch remains.

"You look fine." Nancy straightens my covers.

"Then I'm ready." I sit up straighter.

In a few moments, our team's pitcher Quinn, first baseman Dave, and Coach Paul stride in. As the team's catcher, I've worked most closely with Quinn, and we hang out a lot. Dave's cool too.

Paul's been our coach for three years now, and he was a minor leaguer before that. He doesn't make us do anything he can't demonstrate, like stealing bases and sliding into home. This year, our team, the Tigers, was the runner up at district. Next year we want to go to state.

"Hey, Kay, how are ya?" Quinn gives me a fake punch in the arm. Quinn's called me Kay ever since we met.

"Better. Almost ready to go home." I don't know why I worried about my hair. Quinn's blond hair sticks out like a well-used broom.

"Where's Cassie?" Quinn looks around the room and slides a palm alongside his head. He's had a crush on Cassie for a while.

"She left a little while ago."

"Shoot." Quinn plops onto the end of my bed.

Dave grins big, relocating some of his freckles. "Couldn't miss a chance to check up on you. Had to see if you're really sick or just trying to get out of practice."

"Yeah, you know me." I grin. "Always goofing off."

Coach gives me a half smile and pulls something out from his shirt pocket. "We got a li'l somethin' for ya."

He hands me a Ken Griffey baseball card, wrapped in clear plastic. "Right now, the card's not worth much, but in the future..."

The team knows Griffey's my favorite baseball star. I think he's going to be one of the greats. He's already been an MVP.

"Wow! This is great!" I turn the card over and read the stats on Griffey's rookie year. "Thanks, you guys." My throat tightens.

"We heard you were attacked by spiders. That true?" Quinn asks.

"Yeah, a whole bunch of 'em."

"No way!" Dave exclaims.

"Way. Want to see where?"

Dave shakes his head no, but Quinn nods.

I lean my head back, so they can see my throat. Quinn says, "Wow, they really got you."

When I drop my chin, Dave says, "That had to be scary." There's admiration in his voice, but he's turned a little pale.

"I tried to fight them off, but there were too many." I don't tell them how invisible hands plastered me to the floor, which made it even scarier.

Coach smiles and pats my shoulder. "We're just glad you're okay."

"I should return to practice real soon." I pretend to throw a baseball at Quinn. He pretends to toss it back.

"Good to see you feeling better." Coach puts a hand on the back of each of the guys. "But we don't want to wear you out. We'll see you on the diamond, okay?"

"You can bet on it."

"C'mon, boys." He nudges them toward the door.

At the door, Quinn says, "See ya 'round," and Dave waves. I wave goodbye and set the baseball card on my bed table.

My Private Notes. After Session Four with Dr. Chapman.

I tried to contact Quinn and Dave, my baseball buddies, and Coach Paul to verify my stay in the hospital. They saw my spider bites, well, at least where the cream covered them. I found an old phone number for Quinn, but the number had been disconnected. Dave, on the other hand, who graduated just after he turned seventeen, joined the Navy and was stationed on a nuclear sub for two years. I tried to send him a letter but who knows if or when he got it. I never heard back. As for Coach Paul, I was shocked to learn he was killed in a car accident a year ago.

Another dead end.

Chapman's Journal. Still June 8, 1991. The Hospital.

When my teammates leave my hospital room and I'm finally alone, I open Mom's notes again. The next page is dated the winter I was eleven.

December 22, 1989.

"A day after our family arrived at our cabin in the Alleghenies for Christmas break, Cassie and Calen decided to go ice skating."

My chest goes tight when I think about the details of that scary day, which are burned into my memory.

€ € €

I step out of the cabin, my skate bag slung across my back. The porch boards groan underneath me. A blast of winter wind slaps my face, and I suck in my breath. The frosty air scalds my lungs.

I hear Cassie behind me and turn to see her, skate bag across her shoulders, holding the door and screen open for our Huskie pup Fargo, who's already the size of a small bear.

"See ya, Mom," Cassie calls over her shoulder.

"Yeah, see ya." I yank my wool cap over my ears.

"Check the ice before you put those skates on." Mom shouts from the kitchen. "And close the door!"

"Will do." Cassie pulls the door shut and lets the screen door bang against the frame. Fargo jumps and bounces off me. I chuckle.

Cassie grabs the push broom off the porch and rests it over her shoulder.

I sweep my hand in front of me. "Age before beauty."

My sister rolls her eyes. "Whatever. But no snowballs at my back." She clutches the railing and picks her way down the icy porch steps.

"No promises." Not wanting broom bristles in my face, I wait 'til she's halfway down before I follow. Then I too grip the rail to avoid falling.

"Remember who won our last snowball fight?" Cassie leaps off the last step into a snowdrift that almost buries her knee-length boots.

"You cheated!" I wrench off a small icicle hanging from the porch roof.

"Huh-uh. I won fair and square." She twists toward me, flips back her long hair and sticks out her tongue.

Reaching the bottom of the stairs, I bang the icicle against the railing. It shatters into a million pieces.

Hearing Fargo whimper, I turn. Still on the porch, he has a piece of ice stuck to his bushy muzzle and is rubbing at it with a paw.

"Look, Cassie!" I point to the dog. He shakes his head back and forth 'til at last the chunk falls off. Then he hops back to growl at it, like the ice is alive and out to get him. Cassie and I both laugh.

"Come on, boy." I slap my thigh with my hand.

Fargo slides down the slick steps. He runs past me and pounces into a deep patch of snow, burying his nose and snuffling.

A shiny white wonderland lies before us. Branches hang low from their snow loads. My breath comes out in wet wisps.

"You ready to watch me skate circles around you?" Cassie taunts. The fresh powder squeaks under our boots as we walk.

"In your dreams." I thrust back my shoulders and stomp past her into the trees. Unlike the fresh powder, the crusty snow beneath the trees crunches when I walk. The crisp air bites my nose.

When we reach the pond, the size of a baseball diamond, Cassie sweeps the broom from side to side. She moves the snow from the center of the pond to its edges, revealing the untouched ice beneath. Puffs of vapor escape her mouth as she works.

I play fetch with Fargo, using a small branch. After a while, ice forms on his whiskers.

When she finishes brooming half the pond, Cassie stomps hard on the ice at the edge. She jumps up and down with both feet and then kneels down.

"No cracks." She travels out from the edge and repeats this process several more times.

Thrusting the broom handle in my direction, she says, "Your turn."

I heave Fargo's branch one more time into the trees, as far as my baseball arm can make it fly. Fargo races after the stick, while I slide over to where Cassie stands with the broom.

I swish the bristles over the ice from side to side, thinking the faster I go, the sooner we'll skate and the warmer I'll feel.

Fargo returns, his head hung low. He hasn't found the stick. But one look at what I'm doing, and his head and tail pop up. He skids across the cleared ice to bark and bite at the broom.

Cassie giggles.

"No, Fargo. Go away!" I point to the bank where Cassie is wiping snow off a log.

He slinks to the pond's edge and lies down, head between his paws.

"Do you miss your friends yet?" I shout over to my sister as I sweep.

"My friends *and* my playlist."

Mom and Dad decided we couldn't bring any electronic devices to the cabin, including Cassie's Walkman. According to them, we needed to "de-stress and detach."

"Don't tell Mom and Dad," she says, as she sits on the log and removes her snow boots. "But it's been fun playing board games and watching old movies." She grins as she pulls on her skates.

"Your secret's safe with me." I finish sweeping and carefully walk over to where Cassie laces up her skates, and Fargo sulks. I lean the broom against the log and unzip my skate bag.

My sister stands, steadies herself and clomps to the cleared ice, her foggy breath looking like a halo around her head.

She strokes the ice with her blades to build up speed, then turns and loops. The pond is eerily quiet, and all I can hear is the whoosh of Cassie's skates. Fargo hasn't perked up his ears or barked since we arrived.

Pulling on my ice-cold skates as fast as I can, I wonder how long someone would last in this cold. I mean, I've had my gloves off for what?—all of two minutes. As I lace up my skates, I find it hard to focus on anything but getting my stiff fingers back into my gloves.

Skates tight, check. Gloves on, check. Standing up, check.

It's been a year since I last skated. Legs not used to balancing on blades, I wobble and then my skates slip out from under me with the first push. I hit the ice hard, the blow stinging through my jeans.

I scramble to my feet, hoping Cassie hasn't seen me. No such luck.

"Falling already, Calen?"

My face reddens.

As I regain my balance and brush off my pants, I reply, "Coach says it's not how you start, it's how you finish."

Fargo sits up and barks, like he wants to join us.

"Stay," I command. The last thing we need is a dog sliding between our legs or getting cut by our blades.

I push off, left, right, left, right, and slide to a sideways stop beside Cassie. "See?"

We skate round and round, doing spins and figure eights. A normal afternoon at the skate pond, right? But here's where things get weird.

Fargo starts barking and growling, focusing on something at the other side of the pond. And then he stops, mid-bark.

"What's wrong with him?" Cassie asks.

The dog's jaw's moving, but he isn't making a sound. Maybe he's too cold to bark. Can Huskies even get cold?

"Probably a squirrel." I shrug. I don't see anything on the other side of the pond. But I speed-skate over to investigate, leaving Cassie in the middle of the ice.

Cassie shrieks. I look over my shoulder, and she's gone! My heart races. *Where'd she go so fast?*

"Heeeelp!" Her head bobs above the surface of the pond.

She's fallen through! But why didn't I hear the ice crack?

I hurry back to her. When I reach the hole and drop to my knees, she disappears below the water again.

The weirdest part. The ice is melting around the edge of the hole, not cracking, not sluffing off – but melting. In below-freezing air!

I have to scoot back as the hole enlarges. I can't get as close as I want, or risk falling in.

I've *got* to get her out before she freezes!

All of a sudden, Fargo barks again.

"Go—get Mom." At first, the dog ignores me and continues to bark at something at the far end of the pond.

"Go! Get Mom and Dad! Now!" I yell at the top of my lungs. At that moment, I don't know what I'm thinking. For sure, Fargo is a smart dog. But can my puppy really understand what I'm telling him?

He takes off at lightning speed anyway.

Cassie's head bursts above the surface again. She coughs and sputters through bluish lips.

"I'm going to get you out of there." I tell her, but I really have no idea how to do that.

My heart pounds so hard I can barely hear the voice in my head. *"Get her to kick to the edge. Remember the broom."*

I stare into her terrified eyes. "Swim to the edge of the hole, and I'll be right back." I skate over to the broom, which still leans against the log. I hate leaving her, even for a second. But trying to pull her out without me getting near the damaged ice seems the safest option.

Broom in hand, I skate back to Cassie and stop well short of the ice hole. Cassie makes it to the edge and is trying to pull herself up, but she keeps slipping back in, even though the edges aren't melting anymore.

Dropping to my knees a few feet from where she's fallen in, I dig my toe picks into the ice and, once I feel secure, thrust the bristle end of the broom toward Cassie. "Push yourself up and grab the broom. I know it's hard, but you have to."

She lunges for the broom and falls short. She slides back underwater. Last summer, Mom said we could cannonball into the pond but not dive, so I know the water is at least over her head.

I shoot a prayer upward. "If anyone is listening, we need help."

And then another unexplainable thing happens. She gets a push from below.

That has to be what happens because she appears to defy gravity and leap upward. I can't imagine, as stiff and cold as she must be, she could do it on her own. I imagine a large fish or a mermaid helping us.

She clutches the broom with both hands, but, because she's wet and stiff, I'm worried the bristles will slip right through her gloved fingers. But when I pull with everything I've got, she hangs on.

Slowly, she rises out of the water, groaning with the effort. My muscles shake and threaten to give out, but I drag her, bit by bit, away from the hole.

Finally, she clears the damaged area by a few feet. "You can let go," I reassure. "You're safe now." But she continues to grip the broom.

I pull the broom closer, sliding Cassie along with it. When she reaches me, I have to pry the bristles from her hands because her gloves have frozen to them. She shakes so hard her teeth chatter.

For her sake, we have to get off the ice – fast. "Let's go, Cassie." But she doesn't move. On my now-numb knees, I grab under her arms, bringing her to her knees to face me, careful of our sharp skates.

I'm already so cold I can't feel my fingers or toes. How cold is she?

"I-I-I- ch-ch-checked th-th-the ic-c-c-ce." She shivers and drips icy water on me.

"I know. It seemed solid." I rub my hands up and down her wet, shaking arms. Strangely, she warms up quickly and soon steam rises from her coat and hat.

About this time, Mom and Dad, along with Fargo, come running through the trees at the pond's edge.

Here's where Mom picks up the story.

Chapter 7

<u>December 22, 1989. The Pond.</u>

"The kids are gone for about an hour when suddenly Fargo appears at the front screen door, barking and scratching.

"I let him in with 'What's wrong, boy?'

"He yips and clamps onto my pant leg, pulling me toward the door."

So Fargo did understand me.

"I figure the kids must be in trouble. My heart thrums. Have they fallen through the ice?

"Dragging the dog along, I don my coat, boots and a pair of Mort's gloves, the only ones that fit over my bandaged hand.

"Earlier in the day, I decided to make a pine-cone wreath for our door. As I gathered cones under a thick stand of trees, where the snow was scarce, I reached around a strange,

purple-leafed plant sticking up through the snow. I know this sounds impossible, but it reached out and slashed my hand with its sharp spines.

"Like my ears had just popped and I'd walked into a very bright room, my senses were suddenly magnified. I heard the rustle of the slightest breeze and the shuffle of snow as small creatures scurried about. The green of the trees and the white of the snow were so intense they hurt my eyes, even with my sunglasses on. I could smell the tangy wood smoke from our cabin's fireplace as if I were standing right next to the fire."

Freaky.

"When I returned home, I cleaned and dressed the burning, itching wounds. Worried the plant was poisonous, or possibly hallucinogenic, I perused every book in the cabin on forest flora but couldn't find any information about a weird purple plant that could thrive, even in a frozen forest.

"Back in the present, I carefully slip my husband's glove over the bandage. While he's let go of my pant leg, Fargo continues to bark frantically and zip around in tight circles.

"I open a window and call out to Mort, who's chopping wood. Trying to keep the panic out of my voice, I yell, 'Fargo's going crazy! Something bad must have happened to the kids. We need to get to the pond—now!'

" 'I'll bring some rope and the stretcher, just in case, and meet you out front.' Last summer, my super cautious husband built a stretcher out of canvas and wood saying, while he hoped we'd never need it, it might come in handy if any of us got hurt in these isolated mountains.

"I grab a bunch of blankets from a closet and pick my way down our icy porch stairs, while Fargo bounds ahead.

" 'Heel!' I yell at him. He comes back and walks beside me.

"The effects of the strange plant haven't worn off yet, and my senses are overloaded. The frosty air nips at my neck, distant birds chirp loudly, and the smells of moss and newly fallen snow are overpowering. I shield my eyes from the sun's reflection off the brilliant white landscape and put on my sunglasses.

"Mort joins me outside, pulling the homemade stretcher behind him, a coil of rope slung over one shoulder. I throw the blankets onto the stretcher.

"With Fargo leading the way, we hurry through the snow without speaking, my stinging cheeks reminding me how dangerous this freezing wilderness can be. My thoughts and prayers center on Calen's and Cassie's safety, but my enhanced senses detect the snow crunching under my feet and the brushing sounds of greenery being moved aside, as well as my drumming heartbeat and labored breathing.

"Fargo begins barking as we emerge from the trees by the pond where the kids skate every chance they get. They're kneeling on the ice near a wide, watery hole. Cassie's soaking wet and shaking uncontrollably. Yet steam rises from her body.

"She's fallen in.

"I scream, 'Cassie!' and hurry to her side as quickly as I can, careful not to take a tumble on the ice.

"Mort follows with the stretcher and blankets. While Calen changes from skates to snow boots and Fargo lies down next to Cassie, I grab a blanket, wrap it around her and rub her arms.

"I'm distracted, however, by raised voices at the far side of the pond. I stare at the scene dumbfounded, chilled more by what I see than by the winter air.

"I rub my eyes and blink. 'Does anybody see that?' No response.

"Is the weird purple plant still causing me to hallucinate?

"After Calen and Mort lift Cassie onto the stretcher, I wrap her in blankets. Her lips are blue, and I know we have to get her out of the cold.

"But I can't help but turn my attention toward the strange scene at the edge of the pond where two hooded and robed figures —one black, one white — seem embroiled in a duel."

Part of me doesn't want to know what my mom saw. But the other part can't stand not knowing why weird stuff happens to me and now to my family.

I force myself to be brave. As G once told me, "If you don't face your fears, they'll eat you up."

"As improbable as it sounds, sparks crackle and fly from the sticks they're holding, which must be magic wands. Magic snaps reverberate through the trees.

"The white-robed figure is edged in glistening light, while the black figure seems to absorb light, its black hood pulled low, obscuring the face.

" 'Don't you guys hear or see anything unusual?' I ask my family. Again no response.

"Even over the cracks of their shots, my enhanced hearing detects their argument.

"The white figure declares in a female voice, 'Galdo, you will leave them alone—now!'

" 'Ha, you can't stop me!' The black figure, Galdo, throws back his hood to reveal a gaunt face and a long, hooked nose. He raises his wand and aims it straight for Mort and the kids.

"I run across the ice toward the black figure.

" 'Where are you going?' Mort asks as he and Calen begin to drag Cassie toward the edge of the pond. I ignore him, determined to stand between Galdo and my family, my arms spread wide, even though my heart is pounding.

"Galdo raises his eyebrows, apparently surprised I can see him, and then sneers. He chants in a foreign language. Dark sparks, like shadows, gather at the tip of his wand, and he points it in my direction.

"The woman flicks her wand, sending golden sparks at Galdo's hand. Her hood slips back, revealing a long, blond braid down her back.

"Galdo drops his wand into the snow where it sticks upright.

"The white figure twirls her wand around and around, encasing the strange man in shiny silver rope. 'Calen will fulfill his destiny. You can do nothing to stop it.'

" 'This boy will not ruin my plans for Fairyland,' Galdo growls. He squirms and struggles, but can't free himself.

" 'To enslave the light ones with your tyranny? I think not.'

" 'He must die!' he insists.

"Twirling her wand over their heads, the woman adds, 'Teleportatio, Bisha Province.' And the two of them disappear, along with the wand that was stuck in the snow."

Back to June 9, 1991. The Hospital.

Reading Galdo's last words over and over, I shake my head. I "must die?" Why? What have I done to deserve death? We've never even met. I know nothing about this Galdo guy, yet he seems to know all about me and my future. He acts like a real guy, but magic like his is only found in fairytales.

Laying the notes on my blanket-covered lap, I realize they've generated as many questions as answers.

Who are these people? And who are the light ones?

They all seem to come from a place called "Fairyland." But I've never heard of it. The teacher didn't cover Fairyland in geography.

Could this Galdo guy also be the monk who attacked Nancy, Cassie and me a little while ago in the hospital? Maybe that wasn't a dream after all.

I rub my forehead. Behind my eyes is the start of a headache, and I feel sick to my stomach. I take deep breaths. I don't know what to make of all this.

A while later, when I'm ready, I pick up the notes and read on.

December 22, 1989. The Pond.

"Shocked at what I've just witnessed, I run to catch up to the stretcher where Mort and Calen are pulling Cassie across the snow.

" 'What were you doing back there?' Mort asks.

" 'I thought I saw something. I was wrong,' I lie.

"As we trudge away, I keep looking back toward the pond where the two mysterious figures stood, afraid they'll reappear at any moment. But all is quiet.

"We drag Cassie back to the cabin where hot chocolate, dry clothes and a warm fire await. Other than a few frostbitten toes, she emerges from this incident unscathed, and Calen is unharmed.

"And it only took a couple of days for the spiny plant's effects to wear off. I didn't tell Mort what I saw because I began to wonder if any of it was real. I still believed the purple plant was responsible for my mind-blowing visions.

"And yet, while I don't understand how a place called Fairyland can exist, such a phenomenon explains a lot. If magical beings live there and if they're out to harm my children, particularly Calen, it's no wonder he's been in so many perilous situations.

"Otherworldly, invisible attacks also clarify why I haven't been able to keep the threats away from my children. I can't see the danger coming.

"How or why Calen and maybe even Cassie are the focus of this Galdo character's wrath is a mystery. It sounds like my son's very existence is offensive to him. If Galdo is real, he's convinced

Calen will thwart his evil plans for Fairyland. I have no idea how that will come to pass, but bravo, Calen! If it's true.

"The scary part is, if all of this isn't a vision, Galdo seems unwavering in his determination to kill Calen. He won't ever stop hunting my son. I pray to God He'll watch over Calen when I can't."

My Privates Notes. After Session Five with Dr. Chapman.

After reading about the pond incident, Chapman stated, "You know that was just an accident, right? Even the notes you say your mom wrote debate the authenticity of what she saw."

I stare at her. "But wouldn't you call what happened to Cassie 'odd'?"

"Maybe, but to believe there was anything supernatural about her fall into the pond or that magical creatures from a place called Fairyland were responsible, well, how does that sound to you?"

I had to admit that somewhere called Fairyland with magical people in it sounded silly, like something a little girl would make up.

But what I didn't tell Dr. Chapman was that I couldn't forget the rest of what Galdo said, especially when I recalled all the attempts on my life.

Galdo believes my destiny is to defeat him, which is why he wants to kill me. Doesn't he know I don't want to have anything to do with him or Fairyland, if such a place exists? If he were here right now, I'd tell him, "I won't interfere with your plans, whatever they might be."

I don't care about what happens to some mystical land I can't see. So why not just leave me alone?

And it's ridiculous to think Galdo is scared of what I can do. I'm no hero. I don't know how to shoot a gun or how to deck someone when I slug 'm.

Chapman's Journal. June 9, 1991. The Hospital.

Now my head really hurts. I rub my eyes and stuff the notes under my pillow. I look out the window as thunder rumbles. A storm is coming.

The curtain rustles, and G strolls into my room. "Hi, young man."

"Hi, G." I sit up straighter.

"You've got color back in your cheeks. When are you splitting out of this joint?"

"Soon. A couple of days."

"Wonderful." G sits on my bed. "We've had some good times this summer, haven't we?" He sighs.

"Yep, and I'm excited to go fishing with you again, at least once before school starts."

"We'll see." He stares at his new digital watch. "I received a gold watch when I retired from the railroad, and it says in my will you'll get it when I die. This newfangled digital watch will be yours too."

"Really? So cool!"

All of a sudden, G leans over and grabs me in a tight hug. "You're a terrific grandson, you know that?" He sighs. "I love you."

"Uh, sure." Even though I know he loves me, he's never once said it. And I've never gotten a hug from him before. A wave of embarrassment flows through me, but it's mixed with pride. "I love you too, G." I pull away. "You all right?" It's not like him to get all mushy.

"Yeah, fine, just nostalgic, I guess. I feel privileged to have known you."

"Ditto," I reply. Why does he sound like he's saying goodbye or something?

He hands me a sack. "Here are your tools and my old watch." He rubs his eyes. "My doctor's visit wore me out, so I'm going home. But I'll return, later."

"Okay, thanks for bringing my stuff. I should be back to normal in a week or so, ready to go fishing again."

"Sure. See ya." Shoulders slumped, G rises from my bed and walks slowly to the doorway, looking way older than I've ever seen him. He seems really down today, and he's usually so upbeat.

"Bye G."

He turns and waves.

After he leaves, I try to figure out why he hugged me and told me about his will. All of a sudden, it hits me. He's just been to the doctor. Did he get some bad news?

Chapter 8

My Private Notes.

In the movies when people are buried, the weather's gray and rainy, but not at G's funeral. He would've loved that bright sunny day, perfect for fishing.

A small crowd gathers under the large tent they've set up on the grass. Mom, Dad and my uncle sit in chairs, along with G's remaining brother and sister, their families behind us. I stand behind Dad, while Cassie's behind Mom.

My grandfather's silvery coffin is covered with a bunch of red and white flowers. But I can't do anything except stare at the cloth-covered deep hole in the ground, next to Grandma, who died before I was born. I shudder when I think how G's free spirit would hate being cooped up. For him to end up in a metal box deep in the ground seems wrong somehow, like trying to corral the wind.

The voice in my head reminds, *"But he's not there. That's just his shell. And his memory will be with you, wherever you go."* That doesn't reduce my ache to see him again.

I put my hand in my pocket and rub across the cold, smooth metal of his railroad watch.

Cancer took him in less than three months, before my fourteenth birthday. Everyone said, "At least he didn't suffer long." Like that's supposed to help. One of my birthday presents was his watch. Happy birthday to me.

I vaguely hear the boring music, but the pastor's words, about how G believed in God and was now in heaven, support how he's not in that box. But G wouldn't have liked all this "fuss," as he'd put it. I silently apologize to him.

We never got to go fishing again. And I hardly saw him before he died. I begged Mom and Dad to let me visit him, and at first, they did. Before we moved, I rode the bus to and from his house.

We talked about all the fun places we'd been and things we'd done, like riding the Ferris wheel and feeding giraffes at the zoo. But then he got weaker and in more pain. Sometimes he wasn't conscious, and Dad said I shouldn't visit him anymore, now that a nurse was staying with him. "Let him rest," he said. And when we moved to Harrisburg, the buses didn't run by his house. I hated how I couldn't spend his last days with him.

Because my grandfather didn't like hospitals, he died at home, a week ago. I miss the way his moustache wiggled before he told a groaner of a joke like, "I named my horse Mayo, and sometimes Mayo neighs." I'll miss how his eyes got bright when we experienced something new together, like the time we rode the Twister, a roller coaster that flips upside down. I'll miss our fishing trips to the lake. I'll also miss how he always listened, even when he didn't agree with me.

I won't forget our rides on the train either. He had a free pass for life, a retirement gift he said, so we traveled by train a lot. He explained how the engines and brakes worked, how the signals turned on and off as we rode past. I learned so much from him about all kind of things.

Strange, I don't feel like crying. Maybe that comes later.

When eighth grade started at my new school in Harrisburg, I couldn't get excited about my classes like I usually do. It won't be the same without G around. After school, I often dropped by his house. He always had store-bought cookies and milk waiting for me, and I'd tell him about my day. A year ago, I decided I was too old for cookies. I preferred pizza bites but never said anything. I loved just hanging out with him.

The last thing he said on my final visit was, "Find out why you were put on this earth and don't let anything keep you from your purpose." I'm still searching for my purpose. Will Galdo kill me before I find it?

€ € €

The funeral finally ends, and people file out of the graveyard. Mom's new church is having us all for dinner, so we drive over to the white building with a steeple on top. I've been to the main service there a few times with Mom and Cassie, but Dad's always been too busy to come.

The food tastes like yucky mush, and my throat is dry and scratchy when I swallow. I finally stop pretending to eat and toss my plate in the garbage.

When my weird cousins want to play tag, I refuse, feeling like I'm in a fog. I can't stand all these people around me and am having trouble breathing. Even Cassie, who keeps putting her hand on my shoulder, is annoying.

I really want to be alone. *I have to get out of here.*

I creep up behind Mom and Dad, waiting for a break in the conversation. Finally, I see my chance. "Mom!"

She jumps a little and turns around.

"Are we leaving soon?"

Putting a hand on my shoulder, she asks, "Did you eat something?"

I brush off her hand. "Uh, huh."

Are you feeling all right?" She reaches up to touch my forehead with the back of her hand.

"Just tired. Can we go?"

"Not for a while." She sweeps hair out of my eyes. "But down that way..." she motions toward the hall, "are lots of empty Sunday school rooms where you can rest, if you need to."

I stare down the hall. Alone time sounds great. "Thanks. I'll be in the closest one when you're ready to go."

Normally, being by myself feels dangerous when unseen forces are out to get me, which is why I made friends quickly at school and now walk home with at least a couple of them. But this place feels safe somehow.

I sidle down the hall and open the first door. Cribs are everywhere. Seeing a padded rocking chair, I settle into it and lean my head against the back. I catch a whiff of something antiseptic-like.

I think about G. I can hear his laugh, see him holding me when I was little and scared, and smell his "Old Spice" aftershave. The tears finally do come, and I close my eyes, too tired to sleep, the drops sliding down my face.

My thoughts eventually travel to the last page of Mom's notes, which I read while still in the hospital.

She wrote about two more "accidents," both last year. One where I was pushed from behind and almost got hit by a bus and another when the brakes on my bike mysteriously failed, causing me to tumble down a steep hill. Right before both, I remembered a cold chill wrapping round my body, like walking into a freezer.

Since I now recognize that my body senses when Galdo is near, I'm super aware of what's around me, especially if I feel cold all of a sudden. But even if I can recognize a coming attack, what do I do then? How can I stop what I can't see? I could run, but where would I hide? Galdo seems to know where I am at all times—at home, at the cabin, camping with G— and when I'm the most vulnerable.

I feel a draft as the door to the crib-filled room opens. I jump up, ready to fight.

Cassie peeks in. "Are you okay? I saw you come in here."

I quickly wipe my hands across my wet cheeks and relax my shoulders. "Fine, just needed to be alone."

"I understand. Sorry to bother you." Sometimes my sister can be cool.

She closes the door, and I resume my seat and close my eyes again.

Chapman's Journal. June 10, 1991.

I'm getting ready to leave the hospital, and Mom and I are finally alone. We're sitting on the edge of my bed.

I reach into my back pocket and hand over her handwritten notes. My heart pounds as I tell her, "I found these in my baby box."

She sighs as she rifles through the pages.

"Why didn't you tell me about any of this? It was stuff ..." I stomp on the floor for emphasis, "I needed to know. I thought I was cursed or something." My face gets hot. "I *deserved* to know."

Mom puts a hand on my leg and looks me in the eye. "I'm sorry I didn't tell you earlier. I wasn't sure you'd believe me." She waggles the pages in the air. "I planned to show these to you, but the time never seemed right. It's all so crazy."

"Does Dad know?" I ask. I've wanted to tell him about all of this, but he might think I've cracked up.

"No." Mom shakes her head. "I haven't said anything to him. As fact-based as he is, he'd find it pretty incredible. I figured he wouldn't believe us, unless he could see what we've seen with his own eyes."

"You're probably right." I sigh, my anger dissolving. "And I might not have believed you either, 'til after the spider and strange monk attacks."

She scrunches her forehead. "What strange monk?"

"Remember the guy at the pond, that Galdo creep? I think it was him. He attacked me here in my room."

"Oh, my word!" Mom grabs my hand. "When?"

"Yesterday, after you and Dad left."

"How'd you survive?"

"Nancy defended me, at least I think she did." I don't tell Mom about the bright light because my eyes were closed most of the time. Besides, I'm not sure what caused it, or if it's even related.

"But the strangest part." I scratch my head. "After the battle was over, everyone acted like nothing happened, as if everything was back to normal. At first, I thought I'd dreamed the whole thing, but now I think it was real."

She squeezes my hand tighter. "I'm so sorry. That must have been frightening."

I fight back tears. I can't cry in front of my mom.

"You know I'll do everything in my power to keep you safe," she adds, "including asking God to protect you."

I swallow hard and whisper, "I know." But I doubt her efforts can prevent Galdo from killing me. And, as for God, what's he done for me lately?

My Private Notes.

After Dr. Chapman read this last entry, she asked me if I could explain why Cassie didn't remember the attack at the hospital, if I was even in the hospital. "Which, of course," she added, "there's no record of."

"I think magic was involved." I leaned forward.

Dr. Chapman blinked rapidly and covered her mouth with her hand. *Was she smiling?*

Dropping her hand, she asked, "Why would you think that?"

"Because the Latin word 'oblittero,' spoken after the attack, means to 'blot out.' I looked it up."

"So you believe Cassie's memories were erased, by magic?" She raised her eyebrows.

"Looks like it to me."

"Why weren't your memories erased?" she asked.

"I don't know."

Does any of this seem logical to you?" She tapped her pen against her lip.

"It may not be logical, but I believe it's what happened."

"And how long have you been studying Latin?"

"Come on." I scowled. "I just looked up the one word."

"Mmm, hmm."

Again she doesn't believe me. Is she right? Is my mind playing tricks on me?

Cassie and I talked again yesterday about our therapy sessions.

"Have you convinced Chapman of anything?" she asked.

"Are you kidding?" I squinted at her. "She doesn't believe a word of what I tell her or what I write. But I'm getting all the weird stuff down on paper, before I tell her I made it all up. That way you can look at my journal too."

"I'd like to read it. In the meantime, I'm going to tell her how you've always been dramatic, telling wild stories at the dinner table. I'll convince her that your magic stories are simply your way of escaping the awful reality of what's happened."

"I guess that doesn't make me sound too crazy." I shrugged. "Think we can persuade her?"

"I think so. But we have to be careful and make the lie convincing. Otherwise, they might separate us. Put you in a home for sick kids or something."

€ € €

Even after I got home from the hospital, I couldn't sleep. I'd lie in bed and shake uncontrollably, while invisible spiders crawled across my skin. The other day I saw a tiny spider on the wall and ran out of the room. My bites have healed, but the rest of me hasn't.

A sudden drop in temperature or a creak in the floor in the middle of the night still makes me bolt straight up and clap my hand over my mouth to keep from screaming. I constantly look behind me, like some paranoid freak, and now carry a pocket knife, which seems dumb. I mean, what's a little knife against a wizard, or whatever Galdo is? I'm going to die, and there's nothing I or anyone else can do about it.

Mom and Dad notice the changes in me. "You've lost weight," Mom says. She spoons more mashed potatoes onto my plate. "You need to eat more."

I push the plate away. "I'm not hungry."

Dad pipes up, "And I don't like those circles under your eyes. Still having trouble sleeping?"

How do I tell him I'm being haunted, or more like hunted?

"Not really." I shrug.

He reaches across the table and squeezes my forearm. "I can sleep in your room for a while, if you want."

I wish you could, but I'm too old to have my daddy keeping the monsters away. And, unless you can become a magician too, you can't stop Galdo.

I do a Cassie eye-roll and pull away. "That's okay, Dad. I'll be fine."

€ € €

Little did I know that everything was about to change. Cassie and Dad were out of the house and Mom and I were in the kitchen. I was at the table doing my homework, while Mom made dinner.

Over the sounds of her madly chopping vegetables, she says with a tremor in her voice, "I had another Fairyland encounter this morning, and I've been dying to tell you about it."

"Wow!" My hands shake, and I drop my pencil. My voice cracks as I ask, "Where were you? What happened? Are you okay?"

"I'm fine. But I have unbelievable news. Brace yourself."

Chapter 9

Feeling light-headed, I take deep slow breaths as Mom begins her story.

"I was by myself in the backyard, pulling weeds." She tosses onions and peppers into the crockpot.

"Something kept flitting around my head. I thought it was a fly and tried to swat it away." She places the lid on the crockpot and turns the knob. "Then a high-pitched voice yelled in my ear, 'Stop that!' I screeched and – "

"What *was* it?" I interrupt, leaning forward and gripping the table.

"At first I thought I was hearing things. Whatever it was moved too fast for me to recognize it, at first. Then it hovered inches from my face, and I realized it was a tiny hummingbird, its wings a blur. That was strange enough. But then it spoke. 'Do not be afraid,' it said. 'I am a friend.' "

I jerk back like I've been slugged. "No way! Are you kidding? It spoke English?"

"Yep, and sixty-two other languages, apparently. Human ones like Mandarin and French, it told me, and Fairyland dialects like Elvish and Pixien."

"Whoa!"

Mom adds, "I was as surprised as you and stammered, 'Are you for real?' I looked around, wondering what the neighbors would think if they saw me talking to an animal?" She laughs.

"The little bird bowed its head and said, 'I am Tener, at your service. Here at the royal command of Fairyland's king.' He zipped closer. 'You are Calen's mom, Eloise, correct?' "

"He knew who you were?" I grasp the table even harder.

"I know. It seems impossible." She nods, then sits across from me. "I asked how he recognized me. 'We know much about your family,' he replied, puffing out his chest. 'Calen is destined to do great things for Fairyland.' "

"I am?" My voice squeaks and I clear my throat. "Did he happen to say what those 'great things' might be?"

"I asked him, but he just made little clicks and whistles. Just when I thought he hadn't heard me, he added, 'Humans. So full of questions. All I can tell you is, I am not at liberty to reveal that information.' "

My chest tightens. "Why can't he tell us?"

Mom places a hand on mine. "I pressed him as to why, but all he'd say was that Fairyland's residents take an oath to keep the affairs of their world secret from the human population. If he hadn't been sent by the king's command, he couldn't have revealed himself. He added that their anonymity is for our protection as well as theirs."

"It's sad that we need protection from one another."

Mom nods. "Yes, it is."

Feeling like a little kid with Mom's hand on mine, I pull away and rub my scalp. "If they hide from us, how come you could see and hear him? I mean, the effects of that spiny purple plant have worn off. Right?"

Mom holds her hand to the light and pokes the place where the plant scratched her. "I asked Tener about that. He said the plant was an omniweed. Apparently, its venom allows humans to see into Fairyland, for a brief time."

"I don't get it." Although her injury has faded completely, I stare at her hand. "If the omniweed isn't affecting you, how could you talk to him?"

"Tener told me a spell had been placed on him. 'If it were not so,' he said, 'I would sound like an ordinary hummingbird, and we would not be having this conversation.' "

She rests her arms on the table and leans forward. "I was afraid to ask Tener my next question because I thought he'd say Galdo was planning more assaults on you. But I had to ask. 'Why *are* you here?' "

"And?" My stomach turns at the thought of how Galdo can appear suddenly, when I least expect it.

"He actually cocked his little head. 'Is Calen distressed by the possibility of another attack?' he asked.

"I said you were trying your best to hide your fear, but you'd lost weight and hadn't been sleeping well. I added, 'He's understandably terrified that death is lurking around every corner.'

"Tener then zipped around in circles to where I couldn't keep track of him. Finally, he hovered at eye level. 'The king says Calen cannot be in less than optimum physical condition. And we can*not* allow these attempts on his life to continue.' "

The idea that Fairyland's king wants to keep me safe makes my stomach go from churning to doing flips, like when I rode the roller coaster with G. My heart pounding, I lean close to Mom. "Tell me the king has a solution."

"According to the little bird, the king has decreed that you are to be guarded day and night by the bravest of Fairyland's warriors."

I do a drum roll on the table. "Cool! Who are these warriors?"

"After making little clicking noises that sounded like chuckles, Tener blinked and said with great formality, 'I am not at liberty to reveal that information.' "

I groan. "But, if they're hummingbird size, they won't be able to overcome Galdo."

"Don't worry. After he darted close, the hummingbird whispered, 'Trust me. They are some of the biggest and most powerful creatures in our realm, much, much bigger than I am.' "

"That's a relief." I grin.

She grins back and then sets her mouth in a line. "However, he added that, like angels, you won't be able to see them."

I sigh, wishing I *could* see them. Still, knowing I'm being protected by supernatural beings, even invisible ones, lifts a heavy weight off my chest. I feel like I could fly to the moon and back.

That night, I eat all my dinner and sleep better than I have in weeks.

Chapter 10

Chapman's Journal. October 31, 1993.

The rest of my fourteenth year is my best yet. No more scary attacks and no more crazy Fairyland visions. I almost forget to look over my shoulder. After a few months, I don't carry a knife anymore.

Before we move, I finish the season with my baseball team, the Tigers, who go to state. After we lose a close game to the first-place team, the Pirates, I catch two balls at home plate that kept the Bruins, the third-place team, from beating us. We come in state runners-up and receive a humongous trophy.

The guys put me on their shoulders, and their cheers still echo in my head. "Calen, hooray! Hip, hip, hooray!"

After we move, I meet a girl named Cindy, who doesn't think I'm weird. She loves baseball and doesn't mind working on watches either. Together we have a blast fixing a few of my classmates' timepieces.

I begin to feel like a normal guy my age.

But I should know by now that my being safe isn't meant to last. Shortly after I turn fifteen, my life changes forever.

Crazy how Halloween, the Day of the Dead, is the last day I remember feeling protected. Protected, that is, 'til night falls, and the darkness is able to hide evil in all its forms.

Here's what I remember from that time, which isn't much:

Cassie, who's turned eighteen, invites me to tag along with her to a Halloween party, telling me, "You need to get out more."

"Maybe." I shrug. "But I have tests on Monday, in both science and math." Cassie knows I want to graduate at the top of my class in a couple of years, but she thinks, with 200 seniors at Harrisburg High, that's unlikely.

"You know what Mom says, 'All work and no play...' " She gives me a little punch in the shoulder.

"Yeah, yeah. Just call me a dull Jack.... Maybe next time."

Downstairs, Mom and Dad hand out treats to what seems like tons of kids, while I study upstairs.

After a few hours, I realize the doorbell has stopped ringing, and the house is eerily quiet.

I look at the clock to discover it's past midnight. My parents must be dead to the world.

Feeling like my brain is fried, I drop into bed and fall asleep right away.

The next thing I remember, I'm on our front lawn, watching our house burn.

My Private Notes.

The shrink said, "It's not unusual for our minds to block out traumatic events. In our next session, I want to hypnotize you, with your permission, of course. You'll remember more, and unless you believe a lie in your conscious state, it'll be the truth. This could be a major step in your recovery." I hoped she was right.

While I was under hypnosis, the doctor recorded the following about that awful night, November 1, 1993, and then played it back to me:

My eyes feel gritty, and I can't open them. But I seem able to float above my bed.

No, wait. I'm not really floating. What feels like large hands support me.

The air is hot, burning my cheeks and arms. Noises like rifle cracks batter my ears. Smoke fills my lungs, and I have a coughing fit.

Those unseen hands must carry me out of my room because the door creaks open and what sounds like heavy boots clop on the wood floor of the hallway. I'm tipped forward and angled head down over our wide, curving staircase. The rate of boot clops slows. Soon after, I'm level again, and the cooler air smells clean.

The front door slams shut and then the outside wind hits me, crisp and cold. Boots thump across our porch.

Now I'm lying on hard ground and icy grass tickles my bare forearms. I shiver, wishing I had my coat. My coughing subsides.

My ears are filled with loud roars and lots of popping and crackling, like I'm in the middle of a violent thunderstorm. Bright lights flicker through my closed eyelids.

What am I doing out here? And where's everybody else?

I rub and rub my eyes. Finally, after what seems like forever, I'm able to open them. I sit up, but my vision is blurry. My eyes burn and my nose fills with the smell of smoke. My throat is dry and scratchy.

Of course, I'm not in bed anymore. I'm sitting in the middle of our front yard in my PJs. As my vision clears, I can't believe what I'm seeing.

Our house is on fire!

Is this for real?

Orange flames and black smoke shoot out the second-story windows and into the clear night sky with its round moon, making it as bright as day. It looks like the air itself is burning. A wave of heat hits my face, reminding me of what Mom told me hell is like.

Wood splits and burns, hissing and crackling like cellophane, accompanied by a roaring wind, as the hungry fire devours everything we own.

I scoot backward, trying to distance myself from the nightmare. The rumble of thunder, rare for this time of year, makes me look up as the moon disappears behind clouds. Rain mixed with snow douses my face.

Emergency sirens wail in the distance.

I jump to my feet. Where are my parents? And Cassie? Did she get back from the party?

My bare feet slip as I dash frantically back and forth across the wet grass. I slide into the side fence and, pushing dripping hair from my forehead, peer over the fence. Maybe they got out the back door. "Mom! Dad! Cassie!" I cry. I don't see them anywhere.

I spy the empty dog run alongside the house and am grateful Fargo is no longer on this earth to see this, having died of early-onset cancer a few months ago.

A coughing fit starts again and then an all-out panic attack.

I drop to the ground, drenched through and through, as the world spins and my heart races. I throw up yellow gunk on the soaked lawn.

When the attack subsides, I race toward the front porch but slam against an unseen force, like an invisible wall.

I fall hard onto my back, and air feels like it's being sucked out of my lungs. A loud crash causes me to look up. Our roof crumbles and sinks into the house. The fire's roar intensifies.

This has to be just another nightmare.

On my hands and knees, I crawl toward the house, but bump up against the invisible barrier I felt before. I shove my shoulder against it again and again, but can't get any closer. I stand up and pound on the "wall," screaming, "Let me through! Let me through!"

Collapsing to the ground, I don't stop the tears, which mix with the rain and snow on my face. Sirens now blare in my ears.

I turn from the fire and swipe at my wet forehead. I start shivering and can't stop.

Two howling fire engines and an ambulance skid to the curb. The engines' doors fly open, and several men in heavy suits jump out, pulling giant hoses off their trucks.

All of a sudden, Emily, our neighbor and a grandmotherly type, is by my side. "Are you all right?" she yells over the wailing sirens. She helps me stand and puts something warm over my shoulders.

The sirens stop, and I croak through a dry throat. "My parents! And Cassie. Did you see them?" I cough again.

"No, not yet." She wraps an arm around me, but I push her away.

Another arm encircles me. I start to push it away too, but a familiar voice says, "Calen, I'm here."

Illuminated by the fire's light, a pale Cassie stands close, her eyes wide, her breathing shallow.

I grab her and hug her harder than I ever have before. I whisper in her ear, "You weren't in the house?"

"No, I broke curfew." She hugs me back and then grabs my shoulders to look me in the eye. "How did the fire start? And where are Mom and Dad?"

Words tumble out of me, like rocks down a hill. "I don't know what happened, how I got out, or where Mom and Dad are. You don't think …" My throat tightens, and I start coughing again. My knees buckle.

Cassie grabs me to keep me from falling. "Maybe they escaped in time."

Two guys in white uniforms rush over to us. "Are you two all right?" Cassie nods.

I want to scream, "No! I'm not all right!" But I know they can't do anything to help what I'm feeling.

One of them asks, "Were you in the house?"

Cassie shakes her head, and I barely dip mine.

"What's your name?" the uniform asks me.

"Calen," I manage to whisper.

"Okay, Calen, we're going to take you to the hospital and get you checked out."

"No!" I squeak out and shove the hands away that are reaching for me. I cough some more. "I'm going to stay here!"

"You should go with them." Cassie turns me toward the ambulance.

"At least let us monitor your pulse and breathing over there." The uniformed man points to the open back door of the ambulance. Near there a crowd of people has gathered. *Are they our neighbors?*

One of the medical guys grabs my arm to help me, but I shake him off. I'm barely keeping it together, and for some reason, I don't want anybody but Cassie touching me.

I stagger over to the red flashing lights.

After the medics put me on oxygen, I feel better. I let them check my breathing and heart. They tell me I should admit myself into the hospital if I develop chest pain, cough up blood or get a headache. I promise I will, while really thinking, "Unless I'm dying, there's no way."

Epilogue

Following the hypnosis session, I remember feeling surprisingly peaceful. That was a first because up 'til then, I'd felt so much anger. That house fire may have burned up much of what I loved, but the fire inside me threatened to destroy everything else. Later, when I snapped at Cassie over some little thing, she asked, "What are you so mad about?"

Where do I start?

I was mad at God for allowing the fire to happen in the first place. If there is a god and if he's so all-powerful and all-knowing like Mom believed, he knew about the fire ahead of time. Why didn't he stop it?

I was mad at Cassie for not being there that night with the rest of us. Was her party really so important? Maybe, if she'd been there, she'd have gotten my parents out.

I know it sounds stupid, but I was even mad at my parents, for leaving me orphaned. They were my guardians, assigned to protect me. So why didn't they wake up and fulfill their parental duty? I could have died too.

The craziest thing I was mad at was the fire itself. That cruel blaze not only burned up my parents and our home, but also torched my normal life. If we'd bought a new home instead of an old one with faulty wiring, which the firemen said had to be the cause, they'd still be alive.

But most of all, I was mad at myself for sleeping so soundly. Shouldn't I have been able to save my parents?

Dr. Chapman said working through anger is part of the grieving process. "If you don't face your anger, you'll never get past it. You'll never heal."

How did she know I was angry? Was it that obvious? I never told her what I was feeling, but somehow she knew.

The doctor praised me for my clear recollection of the night of the fire. "But you must realize, an anonymous good Samaritan or two were the ones who carried you down the stairs and outside." She cleared her throat. "And, as for the invisible wall, that was caused by neurogenic shock, where your blood flow and nervous systems shut down from an extreme emotional disturbance, which made you feel like you couldn't move."

I didn't argue with her, even though I knew that wasn't true.

After the fire, Cassie and I spent the next couple of weeks with our neighbor Emily, who had a spare bedroom and couch. For the first few nights, I didn't sleep much because my lungs felt heavy, and I kept coughing most of the night.

There's a lot I didn't tell Dr. Chapman about that tragic Halloween, like how, the next morning, the small voice in my head stated, *"Measures have been taken to make Galdo believe you died in that fire. He won't bother you anymore."*

But that didn't stop my nightmares. After the firemen put out the blaze, they found my parents' bodies, still in their bed, on the second floor, which had collapsed onto the first floor.

When I first found out the people who loved me more than anyone else in the world were gone, I couldn't say or do anything. Just stared off in dazed silence, as my mind leapt across a million questions. The first ones were selfish, which made me ashamed. Like, what were Cassie and I going to do without parents? Who'd take care of us? Where would we live? Even silly ones like, what will I wear to school? Will my homework be counted as late?

My next questions focused on how they died. Were they beyond terror in those last moments? Did they feel the flames? Dr. Chapman told me they probably succumbed to smoke inhalation long before the fire ever reached them. But that didn't do away with my endless loop of bad dreams.

The dreams always start in their bedroom. As flames lap up around us, I can't move, helpless to rescue them. I'm forced to watch their skin melt off their bones. In between screams, they tell me they love me. I wake up shrieking every time.

A few days after the fire, a social worker named Bonnie, a chubby little woman with lots of eye makeup, visited us at Emily's house.

"Calen," Bonnie said, "because Cassie is eighteen, she can live on her own. But you're a ward of the state until you reach your majority. Is there an aunt or uncle you can live with in the meantime?" One of her dark eyebrows arches.

I thought about my weird cousins and how miserable I'd be if I had to live with them, separated from Cassie. Moving again? Starting the friend-making business all over again? No.

"Do I have any other choices?" I asked her. "Can't Cassie and I stay together?" I'm sure I sounded desperate.

"Well, there *is* one way." Bonnie consulted her files. "If Cassie fills out the proper paperwork and registers with the state, she can become your legal guardian. But that process involves finding a place to rent and her being able to support the two of you. The state will also require each of you to start therapy in a few weeks, once you get settled." As it turned out, six months passed before we got in to see Dr. Chapman because the system was backlogged.

"I already have a job," Cassie told her. "I got it right after graduation, to help pay my way through night school."

"What do you do?" Bonnie tilted her head.

Cassie sat up a little taller. "I'm a receptionist at a dentist's office. I'm also studying to become a dental hygienist."

Bonnie scribbled some notes and then looked up at Cassie, her glumpy black lashes blinking rapidly. "Can you support the two of you on what you make?"

"I think so." Cassie tossed her head, her long hair escaping over one shoulder. "Our lawyer called and told me we'll have an insurance check arriving in a few weeks to cover the loss of our home. He also said that Mom and Dad had life insurance policies. I'm pretty sure we don't need to worry about money."

"So do you two want to try and make it on your own? It won't be easy." Bonnie gazed from one of us to the other.

For me, it was the only solution. "I'll do whatever it takes," I stated firmly.

"Me too." Cassie nodded.

At the time, I believed Cassie felt like I did, that staying together was the most important thing. Somehow the family who remains means so much more when everything else has been lost.

For over four years, we lived together in a tiny two-bedroom apartment while Cassie worked and finished school, and I started college.

We sold the land on which the house had stood. No way were we going to build again on that site. Too many bad memories.

People from Mom's church were very generous and gave us furniture and clothes, as well as several months of food, while we waited for all the insurance money to roll in. Things came together for us, at least on the surface.

I finally did convince Dr. Chapman that I made up all the supernatural stuff, that I was "wigged out" by my external reality (I read that in a pop psychology book from the library, and she liked the way I worded it, nodding with a "Yes, yes.").

I told her my panic attacks and nightmares had stopped, which was a lie, but she accepted it and decided I no longer needed therapy.

Her final clinical assessment: "In your past state of horror, your thoughts and actions became disconnected from reality because of feelings of vulnerability, the famous 'flight or fight' phenomenon you've probably heard about. That's why you made up events and people."

I agreed and pretended she was right, even though her analysis didn't explain Mom's notes, which burned up in the fire, or the attacks on my person, both by spiders and Galdo.

After we received the sizeable fire and life insurance checks, the rest of Cassie's education was paid for. The remaining chunk of money allowed me to attend college. I decided to study mechanical engineering.

While I didn't make class valedictorian, as salutatorian I received some good scholarships to attend any Pennsylvania university. I chose Harrisburg Community College for two years to complete my general classes, so I could live at home, actually our apartment. Then I transferred to Penn State to finish the four-year degree, partly because Harrisburg didn't offer a mechanical engineering major and partly because Cassie got married. I didn't want to be a third wheel.

Working part-time in my last two years of college helped with living expenses. I found a job repairing bicycles, and they tailored my work hours to fit my class schedule.

Update: May 15, 2000.

In my cap and gown, fake diploma in hand, I make a funny face at Cassie, who's taking way too many pictures. The university tells me they'll mail my "real" bachelor's degree in a few weeks. I wish Mom and Dad were here to see it.

When I think of my folks, the sharp jab in my chest, which used to double me over, has become a dull ache. I don't think the pain of their loss will ever go away, and that's okay. I don't want to forget them.

While my life will never be the same, that doesn't mean it's over. And I think they'd be proud of what I've accomplished.

But I'm still full of regrets. Why didn't I say I love you more and offer them more hugs? I was just another proud teenager, who wanted so badly to be grown up. When really I was just a little kid, craving to feel his mom stroke his forehead one more time.

Cassie says we never really appreciate people 'til they're gone. I think she's right. I wish I would have told them at least once what they meant to me. Why'd I wait?

€ € €

Postscript: Much, much later, Tener, one of the royal hummingbird messengers, told me the following story in great detail to help me understand my memory loss and the disappearance of my journal.

This scene takes place in Fairyland at Aubrey's, the fairy king's, castle.

I flew in behind Silvermist, the king's assistant, when she entered the throne room. Light filtered in through tall, narrow windows on either side of the gilded and red-tufted throne on which Fairyland's white-headed king, Aubrey, sat. The king's chin rested on his chest and his eyes were closed. His skin glittered like gold.

Silvermist cleared her throat. 'Your majesty, Tener has arrived with a message from General Pholas."

The king's head popped up. "Thank you, Silvermist." He pulled his long purple robes, edged in pristine white, around him and sat up straighter.

Silvermist, who's smaller than the king and whose skin glimmers like silver, bowed low. Her fairy wings caught the light and glowed in rainbow colors that matched Aubrey's larger wings. She retreated through the enormous throne-room doors, also etched in gold.

I was excited to relay my message, so I zipped back and forth in front of the king. I'd cleaned my feathers and dressed in my best blue-velvet vest for this royal occasion.

"Your Majesty." I bowed my head. "It is good to see you again."

The jewel-encrusted crown on the king's head dipped slightly to acknowledge me. "Good to see you too, Tener."

The king leaned forward. "So is the news good from our Centaurian commander?"

"Oh yes, sire." I hovered in front of him. "General Pholas says Calen is still safe and well. As you remember, our Centaur warriors not only rescued him from that house fire after they sprinkled his eyes with pixie dust, but they have also been keeping an eye on him."

"Yes, and how is our young man doing?"

"As well as can be expected, under the circumstances. The humans sent him through mental and emotional counseling. He has finished that program, gone to college and received training."

"Combat training?" The king's voice rose with excitement.

"No, sire. The Centaurs tell me he was educated in something called mechanical engineering, whatever that is."

The king stroked his long white beard. "And, after all this time, is Galdo still unaware that Calen is alive and well?"

"Yes, Your Highness. The sorceress's potion, the one that plants false memories, continues to work. Galdo still believes he succeeded in killing Calen in that fire. But he has been wreaking havoc all over the realm, which is keeping the Centaurs quite busy."

"Oh, dear. And how about our measures to safeguard Fairyland's anonymity?"

"The sorceress said she was able to cast a spell over everyone—Dr. Gray, the nurses, Calen's friends, his sister and of course, Calen – so they do not remember any 'supernatural' happenings, including Galdo's appearances and the spider attack. The pixies stole the hospital records a while ago and then took Calen's journal and brought it back here to Fairyland, so Calen could go on with his life. Until the time is right, of course, when we shall return his journal to him." I shook my head. "Humans are so fragile."

"Yes, yes. All very good news." The king tapped a finger on the arm of his throne. "Is that all?"

I flitted around in circles. "No, your majesty. Pholas wanted me to relay to you how the Creator has revealed to him a vision of Fairyland's near future."

I finally settled in front of the king. "Calen is about to take his rightful place in our kingdom."

Acknowledgements

A project like this doesn't depend solely upon the writer, thank goodness. I've consulted others, including my husband, Steve (I love you, honey!), Aubrey and Brendan Bower (my wonderful and amazing grandkids) and beta readers and good friends John Nichols and Kathy Schuknecht, all of whom gave me valuable input on early and late drafts.

A big thank you goes to my critique group, Amber Bennett, Lisa Michelle Hess, Rebecca Carey Lyles, Valerie Gray, Marguerite Martell and Michelle Netten, a bunch of great writers whose insights continue to amaze me.

Lastly, I need to say thanks to my State Farm insurance agent, Debbie Herring, for helping me understand how fire insurance works.

And of course Google, who helped me validate facts about lots of different subjects like black widow spider bites, chest monitors and catheters, clinical assessments, the Allegheny Mountains, etc.

Finally, if you enjoyed this prequel, please write a review. If you didn't, my name is Schnickelfritz McGillicuty, and my book series is called *Why I shouldn't be a Writer.*

62409728R00067

Made in the USA
Columbia, SC
02 July 2019